Pinch of
Naughty

"You give in to temptation often, Eleanor?"

"Never," she answered honestly.

"That's too bad, Ellie," Cyrus murmured.

"Everyone needs a pinch of naughty from time to time…"

GEM SIVAD

Pinch of Naughty

ISBN-13:
978-1523483532
Published by Gem Sivad, LLC

Published by Gem Sivad, LLC

Editor: M. L. Davis
Cover Design:
Selfpubbookcovers.com/FrinaArt

What the Reviewers are saying…

"This is the kind of book which you start and you can't stop reading until you're done…and then you read it all over again — it's that good. ~ *Laura, Two Lips Reviews*

"I loved the book!!! Perfect for lovers of historical romance, it's a book you can read over and over again with the same delight and pleasure. *~Dolce Amore, Booked Up*

"A lovely romance, with characters that will stay with you long after you finish the book. ~ *Barbara, Just Erotic Romance Reviews*

"…an unexpected delight!" ~zz-Reviews, Bookie Nookie Reviews.

Chapter One
Texas, 1887

Cyrus Burke's long strides carried him toward the house and the woman who sat waiting in the porch swing. As soon as his foot hit the first step, she stood.

"My name is Mrs. Lacey. I am a wid…" She paused and licked her lips as if trying to get the words out. "My husband is deceased."

He knew who she was and he knew she was a widow. She was part of Mable Smyth's delivery and nothing came on this ranch without his prior approval. But he wasn't in the mood for disappointment and even though she came in a nice package, from her air of superiority and refined tones he could tell Mrs. Lacey wasn't housekeeper material. *Mable just wasted my time. I'll dock her next load for that.*

He studied the woman in front of him. Mid-twenties, stubborn tilt to her head, determined jawline, smooth, creamy skin—currently flushed from the sun—pale blonde hair and a pair of fine violet eyes mimicking the color of Texas sage.

He'd looked her over earlier in the day when he'd checked the shopkeeper's wagon contents. Mable's human package had ignored him until he'd pointed out that her hat was listing sideways. She'd corrected the tilt and stared silently at Mable's mule instead of speaking to him. Her hat was slapped on straight now and she didn't mince words.

"I would like to apply for the position of housekeeper."

"No." As soon as she'd given him her prim snub earlier in the day, he'd been pretty damned sure she wouldn't suit. But, he admitted to himself, he'd wanted a closer look. He needed a live-in woman who took care of business around the clock, and that included warming his bed at night.

He hadn't found a housekeeper yet who'd worked out. From time to time he paid saloon women for servicing him at the ranch, but they couldn't cook. And it seemed as though none of the females who were willing to clean, wash and mend were interested in shedding respectability to tend to his personal needs.

Mable knew his requirements, so the current job applicant made no sense. The woman who stood before him might as well have worn a sign saying "morally upright and rigid".

"I tried hiring a respectable woman once." The word respectable stuck in his craw, irritating him more. Hell, he'd been forced out of his own bed to take care of business, lest the housekeeper find out and quit. And that was pure horseshit.

"What happened when you hired a decent woman?" Mrs. Prim 'n' Proper questioned him as though she had the right.

He snorted. "After trying to accommodate her ladyship for a month, I fired her and hired Alice from one of the local saloons to take her place." He didn't add that the arrangement had lasted only as long as it took for Alice to get bored, drink up all his whiskey and steal the pearl studs from his cuff links. But his expression must have shown his disgust.

"You have my sympathy for your previous domestic difficulties." She spoke in a conciliatory tone but the tilt of her straight little nose and the way her delicate nostrils flared showed her true feelings.

"Mrs. Lacey, believe me when I say you don't have the skills I'm looking for. Let it go at that." And it was a damn shame too, because her snooty attitude aside, her high, firm breasts and flared hips offered a pretty tempting picture to a man who hadn't had a ride for a spell.

"I am qualified." Mrs. Lacey straightened all five feet and an inch, ready to argue.

"Mrs. Lacey, is this the first time you've applied for a job?" Irritated at her stubborn persistence, Cyrus stepped closer.

"Yes, but I am still qualified." Her chin lifted a notch and a blush tinged her cheeks.

"Just for future reference, first impressions mean a lot. And I'm not impressed with an argumentative female." He watched her swallow. She looked nervous. Good.

"Mr. Burke, with all due respect, you are being shortsighted. You posted a notice advertising your need for a housekeeper. I am seeking domestic employment. An agreement between us would seem mutually beneficial."

"Mrs. Lacey, you might be able to cook. It's doubtful you can dish it up for fifteen hands morning and night, but I'll allow for the possibility. As for the cleaning, if you say you can dust and polish, I'll take your word for it. In addition to those jobs, there are other duties I employ female help to perform. Trust me, you don't qualify."

When he'd gotten the message from Mable that she had a candidate lined up, he'd agreed to meet the applicant. The woman had looked promising—strong and determined, smart enough to manage a house and pretty enough to hold his interest. Now he could see it wouldn't work out and that riled him.

He was tired and dirty, he'd been stringing wire since before daybreak, and he had another section to finish before he could clean up and eat. Widow Lacey didn't look as though she could handle even warmed-up beans and cold bread. Frowning tiredly, Cyrus waved her away as if she were a gnat bothering him. But the woman wouldn't quit.

"Given the penchant for gossip in this county, I'm aware of the additional housekeeping tasks you require. I'm prepared to take on that chore also."

Cyrus knew he'd made the right decision when she reduced coupling to drudgework, calling bed sports chores. Deliberately he merged his shadow with hers, stepping closer until his stature dwarfed her size, expecting her to retreat. She held her ground, tilting her head just the necessary degree to meet his eyes.

He shook his head regretfully, his cock stirring as he caught her scent—some kind of flower mixed with woman. That combined with her husky tones had him contemplating a hell of a lot more than suppertime. "Mrs. Lacey, you're the kind of woman a man marries to get free labor and a pack of young'uns. I don't need either. I pay a fair wage for a full day's work and my housekeepers have night duty too." Cyrus moved away from her to the door.

"I'll take it," she said, pulling an apron from her satchel before scurrying toward him. "I'm ready to get started." Though he blocked the entrance with his big frame, she ducked under his arm, brushing by him as she tied on the scrap of cloth.

"You won't suit. You'll get started, last a day, and quit." Cyrus spoke to her retreating back, startled at how she'd gotten by him so fast.

"No, I won't," she disagreed, sniffing the air and heading straight for the right door. "I assume if I follow the smell of dirty dishes and rancid butter I'll find the kitchen."

Not slowing down or altering her course, she spoke over her shoulder. "The position of housekeeper is perfect." She slapped the door open and held it a moment. "The gossips have also reported you pay your domestic help quite well."

If Mrs. Lacey had been one of the women he bedded on a semiregular basis, he would have been glad to audition her cooking skills. *Audition, hell. Anything she cooks would be better than Slim's meals.* But he couldn't very well usher a respectable female upstairs to try out her mattress skills—not that the sight of Mrs. Lacey's firm round ass going through the doorway didn't tempt him.

Tired of the whole conversation, he decided to run her off and get back to work. "I like my women to have dark hair and some curves I can hold on to when I ride." *That sure as hell ought to put paid to this conversation.*

Although her cheeks pinked-up some, she rolled her eyes and said, "Yes, yes, I know. I've seen them come and go at the local mercantile. Frowsyheaded and plump is your taste. My apple pie will balance that loss. Close your eyes when we have relations."

Cyrus looked at the pale blonde hair neatly coiled at the nape of her neck and let his eyes slide across her body, openly assessing her full bottom lip, slender neck, plump breasts and narrow waist. *Close my eyes like hell.*

"I don't hire long-term and I'm not looking for a wife." He might as well dispel any notion she'd get a wedding out of the deal.

"Why not?" she asked caustically. "It would seem much simpler than replacing your housekeeper so often."

"None of your business," he snarled, glaring at her. Cyrus found himself in the unusual position of being asked to explain himself. Truth was, he hadn't looked that hard. Women were fine for bed sports and cooking. Having a clean house would be nice too. He'd always figured that eventually the right housekeeper would come along and one way or another he'd make the position permanent.

"Never mind then." She shrugged, making clear her disinterest in his marital disinclination, then she cast a scathing glance around the filthy kitchen. "I would like to fill the position until the next pay period. And I am *not* looking for a husband so you are safe from me."

The little woman shuddered and he didn't know if it was at the idea of getting hitched again or because of the state of his kitchen. Probably the latter since single women were always looking to harness a man.

He studied the room. *Hell yes, it's dirty.* He hadn't had time to get to it for a while. Wondering if he could cozen her into staying long enough to wash the dishes, he began his negotiations.

"Mrs. Lacey, I pay once a month and we're mid-month now. I don't think you can handle the job but I'm willing to let you try for two weeks. We'll discuss terms after we've auditioned each other."

"So you will employ me for two weeks to see if we suit. If not, I'll receive payment for my services and we will part company? That seems fair to me." A relieved expression flitted across her face, replacing the snooty disdain.

"Nope. The job is yours until the end of next month if we suit. If we don't, you leave and I don't pay you squat." Cyrus expected her to tell him to go to hell. "Take it or leave it." He folded his arms, indicating he was done negotiating.

"And if we do suit, then I will receive wages for all six weeks?" She inhaled, holding her breath as though waiting for his response.

"Yep."

"All right," she agreed. "I won't need money until the day I leave." Her voice and manner were crisp and decisive, ignoring him as she removed the knives and forks from the rank pile in the sink, stacking them on the counter.

It had been awhile since he'd had help in, and he expected she wouldn't last long enough to clean the dishes. But as he leaned on the doorjamb watching, she rolled up her sleeves and began scraping crusted food from the plates.

"Woman," he said gruffly, "you don't have a clue what you're offering."

She turned her back on him, hiding her face completely and remaining silent.

The petty defiance irritated him. "Mrs. Lacey, you are trying my patience. Go home. You aren't cut out for this kind of work. "

She turned, facing him. "I was married for five years and I'm not unfamiliar with sexual congress." Pragmatically she added, "Whatever your demands, I will deliver."

Cyrus had a lot of demands and they didn't come cheap. *Nor are they the kind of things Mrs. Lacey would know how to deliver.* He liked the way the soap suds showed white against her skin. It made him think of the room upstairs. His cock unfurled, willing to initiate her into some of his games.

He sighed. Dammit, he was already figuring ways to make it work. She looked good standing there flushed from the heat in the kitchen. *Wonder if she'd climb in the tub with me?* Rashly he said, "I've got a water closet and a bathing room upstairs."

She looked relieved. "I wonder if I might visit your convenience."

"It's up the stairs, end of the hall, last door." He scowled at her, his offer grudging. He didn't need a woman like her prancing around his house, invading his privacy. Mrs. Lacey had respectable stamped from the top of her pinned-on hat to the tip of her kid boots. The body in between invited sin and under normal circumstances, Cyrus would be happy to oblige. But morally upright women got paid with life blood, owning a man's stones before it was said and done.

"It's a very well-built house. When I get finished polishing it to a shine, it will be quite lovely." She pounced on his words, heading in the direction he pointed, blotting her job application with flattery.

Grinding his teeth in frustration, Cyrus watched her mount the steps. He'd offered his convenience and she was already formulating domestic plans. Mrs. Lacey promised to be a pain in the neck. As soon as she came back down, he intended to see her gone.

He was thirsty and rummaged in the cupboard for a clean glass while he waited for her return. There were none. By the time she rejoined him, frustration boiled inside him.

Looking considerably less tense, she said, "I didn't realize you were the ranch owner when you came to the wagon earlier."

"Had I wanted you to know, I'd have introduced myself. I like to look over what Mable carts in before I let her unload." He'd also wanted to see how the new woman treated him before she found out he owned the place. He had to admit, she'd been a snooty piece then and she hadn't changed a bit.

"Mrs. Lacey, let's spare ourselves the trouble of getting acquainted. I'll have one of the boys drive you back to town." Mable Smyth was an interfering busybody bringing a woman like the widow onto his land, so he didn't feel bad about getting straight to the point.

"Mr. Burke." She actually stamped her foot to get his attention. "I am here. Your kitchen is in disrepair, your supper is not prepared—what can it hurt to let me try?"

"Anyone ever tell you you're a pushy woman?" he inquired coldly, the palm of his hand itching to tan her ass. She tilted her head sideways as if considering his words.

"No, I don't believe they have. Thank you, Mr. Burke."

He hadn't meant it as a compliment and told her so. "I don't like pushy women. They tend to get upset when I push back."

But damned if a dimple didn't appear in her cheek. He stood, mesmerized by her almost smile, studying her and the deal she offered, enjoying the way she fidgeted under his gaze.

"Mr. Burke, I am eminently qualified for this position. I understand the intricacies of household management and the idiosyncrasies of men." Her smile became supercilious, her chin went up a notch, and the dimple disappeared.

"Is that right?" he drawled, not committing to anything but a couple more moments with the widow.

"You need a housekeeper. I need temporary employment and a place to stay." She enunciated the words slowly as if speaking to an idiot. "Whether we like each other in between seems very trivial to our current situations."

Cyrus thought he heard a hint of desperation in her voice. "What are you up to, Mrs. Lacey? Spit it out." *Great, now I'm going to get female hysterics.* He pressed two fingers against his temple, trying to stop the throbbing in his head.

Eleanor silently acknowledged that Mr. Burke's frown didn't negate his attractive features. His nose, Roman and proud, balanced his high brow, currently creased in lines across the teak expanse — hard as wood and apparently just as thick. She admired the strong chin, craggy features and well-placed eyes.

Instead of meeting her gaze, his glance roamed lazily over her body. Unfamiliar feelings of heat coiled in her womb and her nipples pebbled under her dress. Eleanor blamed it on terror and stood straighter, trying to hide her response. He was an impertinent clod.

His silence unpleasantly reminded her that he was in charge and waiting for her to answer his question. *I wonder what he'd say if I told him the truth. I'm attempting to remove male dominion from my life forever.*

She turned and plunged her hands back into the soapy water. Having something to do, even washing dishes caked with filth, helped clear her mind. He hadn't said no. Well, actually he had — twice — but she was still here. Eleanor racked her brain for the right words.

She needed to say something and the unpalatable truth wasn't a convincing reason to hire her — she had nowhere else to go. When William, her — estranged, divorced? — husband had died unexpectedly, her grandfather had ordered her back to Hartford. Mr. Burke offered a means to foil that plan by unknowingly helping her toward her goal of independence.

The wages she'd earn would be her start — her grubstake, Mable Smyth called it. She was embarking on a temporary career as a paid servant. Having employed them herself, she knew discreet liaisons happened sometimes between staff and family. *I will not let a trivial detail get in the way.*

Eleanor kept her shoulders straight, telegraphing her determination, but she wanted to give in and slump. She was tired. And although the rank smells coming from the sink made her half nauseous, she was pathetically grateful for the odor, hoping it would cover her own.

The lilac scent she'd touched to wrist, neck and bosom earlier in the day had long since been erased by sweat. Her chemise, dampened by the perspiration coating her body, clung to her back, and even her corset felt wet under her dress. Adding final humiliation, her bladder had demanded relief and she'd been forced to beg use of his convenience — a room considerably cleaner than his kitchen. Miserably she thought, *I will not cry. Men hate a woman's tears.*

The room remained silent as she stared through blurry eyes at a particularly dirty pan. She could feel his gaze locked on her form as he waited for her to speak and she tensed, determined to be the pushy woman he'd labeled her.

"I am looking for employment not a lifetime commitment. I am not afraid of work, of losing my reputation or of you." Girding her loins for battle, she turned to face him and stood wiping her hands on a towel as she told him part of the truth.

To have to ingratiate herself with this man in order to clean his house and wash his disgustingly filthy pans was almost too much to bear. But she would do it. She would placate the devil if it meant freedom to control her future.

Mr. Burke studied her closely before he asked, "How did you talk Mable Smyth into bringing you out here?"

"Mable suggested this temporary employment when she understood my immediate need for a place to stay. I am rather good at making confectionary delights—fancy desserts. Mrs. Smyth has kindly allowed me to sell my pastries in her store. It has been a successful venture for both of us."

Mr. Burke rubbed his jaw, apparently pondering the idea before he questioned her further. "So you're a widowed cook and you've decided to become a business woman?"

Business woman—his description made her feel risqué and sophisticated. Eleanor set aside her usual grim despair as the rancher recognized her budding enterprise as an opportunity. Mable's description of him came back to her.

To get to the Burke ranch, they'd started before daybreak and traveled over a rough trail lined with yellowing patches of water-starved grass until they'd reached the huge gate with a sign threatening trespassers. At Mable's direction, she'd climbed down.

"Catch." Mable had thrown a key to her. "It's always padlocked." She'd pointed at the far end. "The gate's hinged so it swings. Just pull it open and let me through, then close it, lock it, get back up here and we'll make some time."

The blockade had glided silently, opening into rolling grassland vividly different from the parched ground they'd left behind. "How…?" She hadn't known what to ask. How could one side of the fence be so barren and the other look like paradise?

"Pure cussed determination and stubborn will mixed with the smarts to see opportunity and grab it. That's how."

Mable's explanation gave Eleanor confidence as she answered him. "Yes. I'm going into business. I agree with Mable. It seems like a very good opportunity."

"So how do you know Mable well enough for her to be recommending your services?" Mr. Burke gave her a puzzled look.

"I've been selling pastries from Mable's shop for weeks," she told Mr. Burke.

The Mercantile had been the last stop on the way to the train. She'd gone into the store to say goodbye, still trying to think of a way to avoid Hartford. Mable had offered her a place to stay while she collected her thoughts and worked out a more palatable solution than returning to scandal and insult.

"Mable has explained that the nearest sweet shop isn't close enough to offer competition." Eleanor braced herself for Mr. Burke's derision. "I intend to convert the empty building next to the Smyth Mercantile into a dessert confectionery."

"You have carpentry skills too?" He scowled at her.

"I don't understand." Eleanor frowned, trying to fathom what he meant.

"That's a shack you're talking about selling out of. It'll blow down before you can bake your first doodad." He shook his head.

"Mable knows the owner. She says he's always open to negotiations and she'll talk to him about repairs."

He grunted a rude expletive and muttered, "I just bet she will."

At first, the notion of an Alcott-Lacey woman becoming a shop owner had seemed ludicrous. But reminding herself that she was betwixt and between, neither an Alcott nor a Lacey, had helped. Until the courts sorted it out, both her status and name were in limbo, so really her plans were no one's business.

Mable's suggestion had planted seeds in fertile soil. This was an opportunity. It made her uneasy, though, that earlier in the day, Mable hadn't introduced the brusque man she now faced. Eleanor would have scurried back to town had she known the arrogant cowboy might be her future boss.

He'd refrained from identifying himself as well. Regardless that she felt as though she'd been manipulated and spied-on by both Mr. Burke and Mable, Eleanor recognized the need to earn money and for a place to hide from the Alcotts when they realized she wasn't returning.

Her thoughts were almost fevered as she grasped at the possibility of her little pastry shop next to the Smyth Mercantile. Hope anchored her. She would be independent and never again let anyone shuttle her over the countryside, hiding her as if she were shameful rubbish. When she was established, she'd send for her sisters. Eleanor forced her lips into an expectant smile, waiting.

"Has it occurred to you that your stay here as my housekeeper might dirty your public skirts a bit and put a stop to your plans to set up a pastry shop in town?" Mr. Burke's question was sarcastic.

"No, it won't," she answered stiffly.

"And how do you plan to explain a young woman like yourself living unchaperoned under my roof for six weeks?" He leered at her suggestively.

"Because of my state of mourning, nobody really knows me in town. I rarely ventured from Uncle Henry's home, preferring baking all day to social discourse. Mable and her clerk are the only local citizens I met." Actually, she'd seen many come and go in Mable's store, but she'd remained hidden in the back room when transacting business, staying out of sight at Uncle Henry's request.

"Uncle Henry?" he asked and waited.

"Henry Alcott," she mumbled.

He pushed his hat higher on his brow, giving her a hard stare. "You're the bank president's niece?"

Eleanor nodded. She didn't like using social status for advantage, but surely being a banker's niece should give her an element of credibility.

"People will believe what they want to believe. Respectability is a matter of public perception and..." She tried to read encouragement in his expression but saw none. Anger unexpectedly took charge of her tongue and Eleanor finished in a rush. "Mable says everyone knows—you won't bed a respectable woman for fear you'll get trapped in a marriage." She tried to keep the hint of derision from her voice but couldn't.

"Is that right?" His lip curled scornfully and he drawled, "You think because you're an uppity-up, I'll reduce the workload, bein's how you're too good for it? Sorry, Mrs. Lacey. I'm hiring a twenty-four-hour-a-day woman and paying top wages for what I get. And what I get is night duty too."

Eleanor drew herself up to her full height, held his gaze and declared, "You will receive my attentions night and day. The townspeople will believe what is presented to them and when I innocently reappear and set up my pastry shop, my respectability will be intact."

So she's Alcott's kin. Funny he didn't mention her visit the last time I was in town. Cyrus didn't doubt her identity though. Henry's wife was a member of the cult of true womanhood and it appeared his niece was cut from the same cloth. According to his information, a respectable female was pious, pure and submissive. He looked at Mrs. Lacey closer—maybe not submissive.

God, she was a temptation standing there, shiny with sweat, her hair escaping the sedate knot she'd bound it in. In a flash, Cyrus covered the space between them, threw his hat on the table and took her lips, drinking her taste and inhaling the scent of lilacs and woman. It was only a matter of time before she went running, so he figured he'd have a sample before she left.

Sliding his fingers through the soft curls at her neck, Cyrus held her head still when she tried to turn aside, pillaging her mouth, giving Mrs. Prim 'n' Proper enough tongue to shock her drawers off. If that didn't chase her away, nothing would.

Apparently though, things in Mrs. Lacey's life had turned to deep shit—she didn't run. She held on to his shoulders as he grabbed her rump, lifting her high and notching his cock against her mound. Then he set about delivering kisses to her eyes, her rigid jawline and back to her lips, taking her mouth with his tongue again.

When he let her go, they were both gasping for breath and Mrs. Lacey's hat hung over her left ear. His voice was a ragged growl as he asked, "You still think you can go back to town looking innocent after six weeks in my bed?"

Fascinated, Cyrus watched Mrs. Lacey right her hat, slide the tip of her tongue across swollen lips as though tasting the idea, then frown as if the flavor was unsatisfying. Deliberately, holding his gaze, she answered. "Yes."

Crowding close again, he grasped her chin and tilted her head to study her. "It takes a lot of nerve for a lady like you to sell her services. Things must be getting desperate if I look like an option."

She touched her finger to her bottom lip as though checking for damage and then dropped her hands to her sides, fisting them.

He thought she might be preparing to take a swing at him.

"Mr. Burke, at home, I am a divorced woman with a ruined reputation bringing shame to my friends and family. In Texas, I am an unknown."

"You lied. You said you were a widow." He tilted her head higher, stretching her neck, his mouth inches from hers as he murmured his complaint. Cyrus sometimes did a little creative engineering with the truth, but it graveled him when others did too. Mrs. Lacey's character got another demerit.

Leaning so close her breath was a caress, she corrected him. "I did not tell an untruth, Mr. Burke. I said my husband was deceased, and he is. I was once the wife of William Lacey and William is dead."

Cyrus' eyes lingered on her lips, enjoying the brush of air she'd shared while trying to best him. For all her starch, she wasn't much more than a girl. *A grass widow, huh? Guess she's right. If her once-husband's dead, one way or another, she's a widow and a woman of experience.* Interest tickled inside him. "How old are you, Mrs. Lacey?"

Her gaze shifted to his nose. That didn't surprise him. He was proud of its prominence. He looked down its length and intercepted her glance, releasing her chin to grasp her shoulders.

He watched her gaze trail lower, stopping on the tuft of hair showing where his shirt opened at the neck. She seemed mesmerized.

"Your age, Mrs. Lacey?" He wondered how long it would take her to answer. Twin splashes of red marked her cheekbones as the simple question seemed to stymie her.

"Mrs. Lacey, tell me your age right now." Damned if a female couldn't turn a straightforward question into a goddamned tussle for control. And the sparring only incited his lust. His cock was at full sail and one taste of her had made him want more.

Wonder if her lower curls are as soft as the hair on her head. He thought of the silk scarves stored in his closet and imagined Mrs. Lacey tied to his bed,

28

spread-eagled and squirming as he trailed feathers across her peach-colored skin.

He studied the stray tendrils on her neck before his gaze traveled up to the hat she was righting. When she finished it was just as prim and tight as it had been when she'd arrived. The lips he'd plundered moments before were set in a grim line and a hint of tears sparkled in her eyes. Sadly he discarded ideas about feathers and fun. All he needed now was for her to start bawling and he'd haul her back to town himself.

Chapter Two

Eleanor couldn't think with Mr. Burke glowering down at her. The truth was, she was fuddled from his kiss. She stammered her answer, bending backward to avoid the nose hovering above hers. "What difference does it make?"

When he remained aggressively close, she said hurriedly, "I am twenty-nine."

He stepped away and Eleanor forced her eyes up from the tanned skin on his neck to meet his wintry glance. *After all that forceful intimidation, my age didn't even matter.* She could see it in his eyes. *It was just a petty show of authority.*

"You satisfied with the pay?" Mr. Burke's voice dripped sarcasm.

Eleanor nodded her head mutely. She didn't know how much he paid but any wage was more than the nothing currently in her reticule.

"Mrs. Lacey, if I let you play at housekeeper for two weeks, slinging hash, scrubbing floors and tending my needs, I don't want any whining about the requirements."

"Thank you, Mr. Burke, I appreciate the opportunity," she said sedately. Aware of the sly gleam in his eye, she tensed, waiting for another sneak attack. He'd already proven himself to be unpredictable and erratic.

"You can audition today. Finish those dishes for a start."

"Uh...of course," she stuttered. "I-I'll do that right now. From the appearance of your kitchen, I've arrived none too soon." Eleanor almost slithered to the floor in a puddle of relief.

She hesitated and then asked, "I have everything I need with me in my satchel. Shall I select a bedroom to use?"

"Suit yourself," he drawled, stepping close again and peering into her eyes. "You have a first name, or am I supposed to keep calling you Mrs. Lacey when we fuck?"

She was shocked scarlet by his crude words. *He's attempting to scare me away again.* Refusing to be baited, she replied primly, "My name is Eleanor. I'll call you Mr. Burke, as any good domestic would." She folded her hands, pretending servile humility, refusing to allow him the pleasure of flustering her more.

He made a noise Eleanor could describe only as a growl and headed for the back door. Before he exited, he picked up his hat and said grimly, "Guess you can figure out what needs done."

Relieved that they had finalized the difficult interview, she offered him her hand. He ignored it, giving her orders all the way out the door.

"Have supper ready at sundown. This place is a mess, so get busy on that too. There's a pile of clothes..."

Eleanor blinked as the door shut, leaving her with what she'd bargained for. She looked around the disastrous filth she'd agreed to clean, hoping the local gossips had been right about the generous salary he paid his housekeepers. *He thinks he'll chase me away before I collect my wages. I'll show the swine!*

Eleanor swept the dirt before her, attacking the task at hand with fortitude. *Pushy? I wish I could beat him over the head with this broom.* She vented her frustrations on the room, removing one layer of grime at a time until the kitchen was clean enough to cook in. Only the lower rooms in the house had been abused. Her quick peek on her trip upstairs had found bedrooms that were dusty but neat and orderly.

It had taken only moments to hang her one change of clothes in a closet, don her work gloves and return to the kitchen. She carried in the supplies, set the canned beans and peaches in the pantry and looked for more inviting food to prepare.

Outside, a garden provided fresh vegetables. The icehouse was filled with smoked meat and rounds of beef. Inside, the pantry held flour, sugar and spices, and she found a basket of semi-fresh eggs hidden under some dirty linens on the counter.

After the meal was organized, Eleanor remembered the laundry he'd mentioned. There were not enough hours in the day to complete all his assigned tasks but when the ranch hands rode into the barn lot at dusk, she felt she had given him his money's worth.

He'd said fifteen hands which meant sixteen employees to feed, counting Mr. Burke. Eleanor calculated the size of portions to be served after considering the brisk intake of William's friends. She'd supervised the preparations of the robust amounts of food they'd consumed.

All was prepared and waiting when the cowboys came through the kitchen. Although she was at the stove with her back turned when her employer walked in, she already recognized his step, his scent and the aura of power surrounding him.

His tread vibrated through the floor, sending tingles of alarm along her spine as he crossed the room and stopped next to her at the sink. The remembered taste of Mr. Burke made Eleanor swallow nervously. As she peeked sideways, he rolled his sleeves to his elbows before lathering, scrubbing and rinsing away grime.

Her gaze crawled from his calloused hands up bronzed forearms, clinging there like lead filings stuck to a magnet. Instead of experiencing panic, fear or disgust, her body flooded with heat.

Cyrus inspected the kitchen before he glanced at her and asked, "Supper on?"

Eleanor resisted the urge to smooth her hair and straighten her apron as he casually studied her appearance. "Yes, Mr. Burke," she replied, as crisply professional as possible.

"Good, I'm hungry." He pitched the drying towel in a crumpled heap on the counter and walked into the dining hall.

For such a brawny man, he moved with an almost sinuous grace. His denims hugged his long frame, outlining strong thighs and the firm bottom Eleanor admired all the way through the door.

As soon as it closed behind him, she grabbed the cloth he'd discarded, burying her face in the damp folds to cool her cheeks and tame her rioting thoughts. *His arms look like sculpted metal.* Eleanor fanned herself with the towel and listened. *I need to compose myself.*

It was very silent in the room. She had anticipated loud talk from the cowboys. William's friends had been increasingly raucous as they ate and drank wine. Of course this was a different setting and coffee was the beverage not alcoholic spirits.

Were they enjoying the sautéed carrots, cauliflower drizzled with hollandaise sauce and roasted beef? She'd garnished each plate attractively with a sprig of mint from her own supplies brought along to decorate her Saturday and Wednesday pastry order.

I will speak to Mr. Burke about continuing my baking for Mable—but not yet. Another conversation with him so soon was impossible. Eleanor stood smoothing the wrinkled linen, wondering about the night duties. *He expects me to renege. Well, I won't. Five minutes in his bed and off to my own. It will be nothing more than a minor irritation.*

Satisfied she had that plan under control, Eleanor focused on the dining hall. Although she strained to hear, nothing more than an occasional clink of cutlery against plates drifted to her. Filled with worry that the meat had been undercooked or the vegetables too done, she carried the coffeepot into the room, preparing to replenish their cups.

Mr. Burke was at the head of the table in a chair fit for his size—*a king among minions.* As one of the minions, she waited humbly for comments on her meal.

"Where's the rest of the food?" When she stared dumbly at him, cold chills rippling through her, he spoke impatiently. "Bring the bowls in here and we'll serve ourselves. From now on, don't be divvying up portions like that. And take this out of here." He handed her the artful centerpiece she'd made from paper and cloth. "Henley tried to eat it."

"I'm so sorry," she whispered. "I didn't allow for the appetites of your men. There is no *rest of the food*."

"Well, damn. That's it?"

"Boys." Cyrus got the crew's attention, which wasn't hard since it had taken them no time to polish off the food, scrape the plates and scoop up the crumbs from the hot rolls. The sample had been worth repeating and now they waited expectantly for more.

"Meet the new housekeeper. It appears she fell a mite short in her first meal. Maybe she'll do better tomorrow morning. Give her the respect she earns and keep your hands to yourselves." He frowned apologetically at the men.

It was the best he could do in explanations. Hell, the drovers hadn't yet forgotten his last cook's shortcomings. Now this. Still, it had been tasty and she'd tried.

He pushed his chair back with a loud scrape, signaling the meal was at an end. She laid a hand on his shoulder, stopping him from rising. "I haven't served the final course."

"I thought the food was all gone." Her small palm resting next to his chin distracted him. He wanted to turn his head and nip it.

"It's just desserts," she explained. "But…" She moved her hand before he could sample it, as though fearing he might take a bite before she could scurry back to the kitchen.

"Guess she's got something else fixed for us. Hold up there, boys, while she brings out her next attempt." Cyrus scooted closer to the table.

"No wonder your housekeepers don't stay long, Mr. Burke. You are rude." Her words were murmured for his ears alone.

"I didn't hire you to teach me manners, Eleanor." He didn't bother to lower his voice when he answered her.

"Mr. Burke, since you are so needy, I'll throw those in for free." Her face flushed and her jaw squared. Mrs. Lacey didn't even try to look chastised.

It had been awhile since anyone had sassed him—probably because he didn't take to sassing well. On the other hand, the job applicant's temper kept popping out like the unraveling of a too-tight corset and he suddenly had an interest in hearing more.

Someone at the table snickered. Cyrus sipped his coffee and waited to see what she'd do. It was suddenly important that Mrs. Lacey wasn't a loose woman. He told himself he wasn't looking for a woman who'd service the whole ranch crew — just him.

"I have dessert to serve." Her eyes remained fixed on the table, not him or the men staring at her. Setting the pot of coffee by his arm, she retreated to the kitchen.

Cyrus topped his cup off and pushed the pot toward the next man in line. His belly growled. They ate twice a day and this had been slim pickings for sure. He looked at his empty plate and frowned, as did every man at the table.

"We'll starve to death if you hire that one, boss." Jake Connelly, Cyrus' foreman expressed the opinion of them all.

"Not gonna happen. I need to eat too. Slim, I'll tell Mable to send out more beans and we'll make do with your meals until I get a fit housekeeper who can cook." Cyrus thought of the sweet skin and soft curves he'd be giving up and then shrugged, indicating indifference he didn't feel.

His strategy worked when fifteen groans, including Slim's, filled the air.

"What the hell's taking her so long?" He wanted her employment to appear in jeopardy, although every whiff of lilac he inhaled made her stay a lot more certain.

He stood, strode to the kitchen door and pushed it open, expecting to see a cake the size of a pigeon egg. The scent of cinnamon and apples hit him first and then drifted into the dining hall, interrupting the grumbling going on.

Her face was pink, her upper lip dotted with perspiration and her expression apologetic when she carried in the tray loaded with apple pies straight from the oven.

She set the tray down and cut the three pies in thick wedges of flaky crust and oozing filling. She left, returning with two chocolate cakes and a pile of something she named éclairs.

Excitement filled the air. Cyrus didn't recognize the name but when he bit into the chocolate shell, cream pudding squirted into his mouth, melting on his tongue before he swallowed. When she set down the bowl of cookies—pecan, his favorite, oatmeal and sugar—he knew he was going to hire her and to hell with what the ranch hands wanted.

Silently she replenished the coffee in the pot and refilled each mug, watching the men anxiously as they devoured the exotic concoctions. Not many had sampled such riches and none, including Cyrus, had ever known anyone who could make them.

"I am terribly sorry to have under-calculated your needs. It's a mistake I promise I won't repeat if Mr. Burke gives me the opportunity to continue as his housekeeper." She'd paused at the door, ignoring Cyrus as she apologized to his ranch hands.

The men licked the tines of their forks, drank fresh coffee and forgave her from sugar-glazed eyes. Reluctantly they stood, filling their pockets with cookies before they left.

Cyrus grabbed a pecan sandy and followed her retreat into the kitchen. Not one to compliment half accomplishments, he reminded her of her lack. "You'll have to adjust your proportions."

Taking a bite of the cookie, he chewed it reflectively before judging it the best he'd ever had. Supper had been half measures, but still… He licked sugar from his lips, savored the pecan flavor and remembered the feel of her soft mouth under his.

She moved him aside, stepping around him, shedding his presence as soon as the last man's departure gave her a reason to leave the kitchen. She paused in her trek to the dining hall to get in a smart remark. "In the future, I'll cook enough to feed a pack of wolves. Then I'll fix more for your crew."

So Mrs. Prim 'n' Proper wants to get snippy. Cyrus smiled grimly. "After you clear up the supper mess, I'll be working on my books at the table. Go upstairs and use the bathing room. I like a clean woman in my bed."

The order sounded pretty rough even to him, but if she was going to bolt he figured it might as well be now. He'd told Jake to be prepared to escort her back to town.

41

Cyrus already knew better than to expect silence. She stared at him, scanning his dirty denims and sweaty shirt.

"I trust you will acquaint yourself with that facility as well." Having gotten the last word, she elevated her nose, telegraphing her pugnacious desire to hit him as she cleared the supper dishes, leaving a clean table for his work.

First the sound of pots banging then a closing door drifted from the kitchen. *Did she leave? I'll be damned if I go looking to see.* Cyrus immersed himself in cattle business, trying to ignore his internal hum as his curiosity prodded him. Just how serious was Mrs. Lacey about this job?

"Mrs. Lacey, here's to our deal." Cyrus poured himself a short shot of whiskey and saluted the missing housekeeper, downing the fiery liquor in one gulp. He checked the clock. The house was silent but it didn't have its usual empty feel. Lips curled in a sardonic grin, he stood and stretched.

The kitchen was warm when he carried his empty glass to the now spotless sink. A peek under an unexpectedly clean linen revealed rising dough. Half surprised, he murmured, "Guess she didn't leave, and the boys will at least have bread for breakfast."

He studied the room. The place looked good and smelled better. She'd hauled away the trash piled in the corner and Cyrus reminded himself to scout around and relocate it to his compost pile.

He put on his hat, went out back to the garden and grabbed two buckets for water. His foreman sauntered up to the pump and began filling the buckets for Cyrus.

"Hope she's got more for breakfast than a cookie," Jake muttered. "Any of 'em left?" Evidently the wave of sugar having faded, the ranch hands were ready to rethink their temporary support for Mrs. Lacey. "We'll give her one more meal to prove herself and that's it."

Jake argued for and against Eleanor's employment while Cyrus watered the melon patch and remained noncommittal. His stomach rumbled its own complaint as Jake mumbled, "Night, boss," and returned to the bunkhouse.

He had favorites among his crew but didn't coddle any of them. He wouldn't keep anyone on the ranch he didn't trust and he paid the best wages in the state, which made his men loyal to the bone. But dammit, they counted on decent food when they pulled a full day's work. Mrs. Lacey was an indulgence he couldn't afford — like one of those fancy cream things she'd served — more air than substance.

It was unusual for Cyrus to be ambivalent about anything. But the woman waiting upstairs made him pause. She was delicate, like an exotic flower, not made for tough housework or rough loving. He shrugged regretfully, making plans to return her to town the next day.

But still—she'd stood toe-to-toe with him, insisting she could handle him and everything he threw at her.

It was late and he suspected Mrs. Lacey was curled up asleep. In spite of his firm belief she was the wrong woman for the job, Cyrus took the steps two at a time, suddenly eager to see what kind of dessert Eleanor had to offer for night duty.

Her scent hung tantalizingly in the air when he entered the bathing room. It was more an essence, a feeling, instead of the heavy, cloying perfume his recent housekeepers had used to cover their smell.

Cyrus stripped fast, scrubbed dirt and sweat from his body and climbed out of the tub. He didn't deliver the usual hand job to appease his hard-on. Instead, he breathed in the smell of Eleanor, thought about her naked and waiting in his bed and just in case things went the right way, rolled a condom over his rigid cock. In deference to her *respectable* status, he pulled on a clean pair of denims, leaving them unbuttoned to ease the pull on his groin, and padded on bare feet to his bedroom.

She'd obeyed orders. Mrs. Lacey—Eleanor—sat upright against pillows and headboard, her hands folded in her lap, waiting for him. She'd left the lamp turned low so he could see the shape of her under the sheet drawn across her lap. Her pale yellow nightgown, although a sedate affair, revealed the swell of unfettered breasts beneath the fabric.

The condom encasing his length tightened around him as his cock thickened. He felt like a stallion ramped and ready to cover a mare as he eliminated the distance between them.

"Ready to seal the deal, Eleanor?" Leering down at her, he leaned over the bed, his palms on either side of her hips.

She grabbed the sheet, securing it tighter around her. Cyrus admired the colors playing over her features. She blinked at him from violet eyes accented by strangely dark lashes and darker brows considering her otherwise blonde hair.

Cyrus licked his lips. She looked as smooth and creamy as one of her exotic treats. He focused on her ruby lips marked where her white teeth had gnawed on the bottom one. Closing the space between them until his nose bumped her flushed cheek, he tasted her mouth, running his tongue along the tightly closed seam before he toppled her sideways off the stack of pillows.

He'd intended to scare the bejesus out of her, proving his point that she wouldn't suit. Instead he found himself sprawled on top of her, feeling every inch of that fine body cushioning his big frame as his chest pressed against firm, plump breasts.

"Mr. Burke." Her words brushed against his lips and he leaned back an inch.

"What?"

"Is this quite necessary?"

That tied it. "Mrs. Lacey, did I not tell you this wouldn't work?" He rolled off her before he lost complete control and forced the issue. Grimly he started for the door.

The ache in his groin wiped out the pleasure in her cookies. He had the door open and intended to put her in the wagon himself and say good riddance to Widow Lacey once and for all.

"Wait, I'm ready."

He knew damn well it was a mistake but he walked stiffly back to stand beside the bed. Without a word, he dropped his denims and stepped out of them. His cock waved in the air, undaunted and ready to play.

"What is wrong with your male part?" She pointed at his erection trussed up like a sausage roll.

"Never seen one of these before?" Cyrus looked down—the rubber was stretched to a thin gold color encasing his cock like a glove.

"No. What is it?" Mrs. Prim 'n' Proper pulled the sheet up to her chin as though afraid of catching something.

"They call them French letters." He watched her head tilt sideways like a robin's, questioning his words. "It's a condom," he said gruffly, not in the mood to explain the device.

"What are condoms?" Eleanor asked in a puzzled voice.

"Cock gloves, rubbers, dick wrappers," he said grimly. She still looked mystified. "It covers me so I won't leave a kid in your belly." Pointing at her nightgown, he growled, "That's gotta go."

The quivering in her stomach spread to her limbs and Eleanor shivered from both the anger in his gaze and her icy terror. Somehow she had lost control of the situation and the reality of Mr. Burke's half-naked presence wiped out any thought of a quick interlude during which she would doze. "My sleepwear?"

"Yep," he growled. "If we're doing it, we're doing it right. Now take it off."

Eleanor stared at his stern expression and saw no reprieve. She pulled the sheet higher and fumbled with shaking hands at the ribbon closing her gown.

As she wiggled out of her nightwear, the sheet slipped, revealing her bare shoulder. A low rumbling sound emerged from the man standing by the bed. Mable's earlier description of him as a wolf seemed only too accurate.

Eleanor lifted the sheet higher, as if its thin material would protect her from the stiff member jutting at a right angle from Mr. Burke's body.

"As long as we're losing things," he said, reaching for her cover, "this goes too." He grabbed the sheet, wrestling her for it until the sound of ripping material and her fully displayed naked body signaled her defeat. "Cost of one new sheet coming off your wages."

Eleanor didn't know what to cover or how to hide. His gaze slowly crawled up her frame, lingering on her breasts. Traitorous nipples hardened into pouting nubs and she clapped her hands over them.

His eyes narrowed into a hooded glance assessing her. Eleanor inched backward until she sat with knees folded under her and arms primly covering her chest. Remembering the voluptuous woman she'd seen at the local store, reputed to be one of his lady loves, she glared at him, daring him to insult her less spectacular curves.

His silence irritated Eleanor so much she decided to be equally rude. She let her gaze play over his naked expanse. Mr. Burke's muscular thighs were connected to strong legs with rope-like tendons showing under the skin.

Eleanor let her gaze rove higher, studying the slim hips, flat hard stomach, broad chest and powerful shoulders. Her eyes traveled upward until she met his gaze and recognized the sardonic tilt of his eyebrow. His expression was relaxed, his mouth curving into an almost smile.

Heat coursed through Eleanor's veins. Hastily she dropped her eyes, stopping at the iron pillar surrounded by a pelt of dark curls at his groin. It moved, jerking as though acknowledging her glance.

"Are you sitting there all night gawking at my dick, or are we certifying our business relationship?"

"All right." She flung herself backward, grabbing hold of the bedding on each of her sides. "I'm ready for your ludicrous night duty." Eleanor closed her eyes, resigning herself to the indignity of coupling with Mr. Burke.

"You look like a virgin sacrifice," he growled as soon as she took her place.

"I'm neither innocent nor sacrificial. If you don't mind, I'd like to get this over with. I have bread rising I need to attend." The idea of punching the air out of the bloated dough suddenly appealed to her very much. She had to open her eyes to glare at him.

"Since I'm the employer and you're the employee and night duty is part of the job, I'll do the prioritizing." He moved between her clenched thighs, parting them easily, looming over her. The last part of his declaration was lost in a grunt as he opened the lips of her sex.

She tensed, counting the hairs on his chest to pass the time.

"You're tight," he grunted.

"I beg your pardon," Eleanor apologized.

"Guess we'll just get this first time over with."

Mr. Burke's words mimicked William's, "Let's get it done," spoken at each of their infrequent visits. William's manhood had been small, popping in for a moment before he sighed, withdrew and bid her "good night" — her cue to return to her room.

Dutifully Eleanor gripped the bedding, anchoring her hands as the rigid end of Mr. Burke's member touched her entrance. She couldn't repress the shudder racking her body. Mr. Burke was not William and his member was not small.

"Let go of the sheet and put your hands on me."

He wanted her to touch him? She didn't know if she could. Eleanor's breath froze in her lungs, making it difficult to formulate her request. "Put the light out, please."

He braced on one arm, muscles bulging as he held himself above her and reached across to extinguish the lamp, clothing them in darkness. "Now put your arms around me."

Eleanor pried her fingers loose from the sheet, tentatively embracing him as she wondered what to do with her hands — leave them cupped or lying flat?

"Run your fingers up and down my back."

She closed her eyes and obeyed, using her fingertips to explore the thick muscles in his shoulders before venturing down his spine. He radiated heat like a hot oven.

"Mark me," Cyrus whispered against her throat, settling his hips in the juncture of her legs.

Mark him? Eleanor focused all the frustrations and anger she'd felt for months on obeying his command. Arching her palms, she made her nails into talons, scratching his back from rump to shoulder.

His hips jerked and she whimpered as his manhood penetrated her like a battering ram, stretching her tight passage, mimicking the exquisite drag of her nails scoring his flesh.

"You're too big." She gripped his shoulders, hanging on as her internal muscles flexed and squeezed trying to stop the molten iron forging toward her womb.

"We're fine," he grunted in response to her complaint.

When she would have protested again, the savage covered her mouth with his, poking his tongue inside as he had earlier in the day. Eleanor's attention divided between the heavy penetrating member below and the thrusting invasion above.

Her fingers curled in his hair. When he released her mouth, she gasped for breath, readying to argue again but… He nudged her head sideways, planting his mouth on the spot dividing neck from shoulder, licking and nibbling there until her dissent became a moan.

Exquisite pleasure rippled through her. Her fingers slid from his hair to his jaw, stroking the rough stubble abrading her skin. The cloak of darkness heightened her senses so that she felt even the tickle of his short curls against her mound. She was filled with him, surrounded by him, covered by him, steeped in the heady male scent of him.

It was not—unpleasant. Pressure coiled in her belly. Prickles of fire danced up her legs, centering in her cleft. She pressed against his groin, tentatively rotating her hips, seeking some kind of relief.

"That's it, play with me." He growled his approval.

His totally obscene suggestion made her channel clench hungrily and she arched upward, seeking more sensation. Again he found her mouth. This time she tried to turn her head, denying his tongue until he shifted his position and began bumping her pearl with his groin.

"Stop," she panted. The feeling was too intense. Horrifying need that was almost pain raked her into frenzy.

Eleanor shoved against his shoulders, trying to twist away. "You're suffocating me."

He came up on his knees, gripping her rump and lifting her to meet his continued thrusts. "There…there…there…" His growls punctuated each tap, focusing her on the spot that screamed for relief.

Wound so tightly she thought she might explode, Eleanor begged him, "Mr. Burke—please…"

Finally, giving into her need, she braced her legs on the mattress, matching the rhythm of his motion, rocking upward to catch his slick rod that pistoned in and out of her.

"Come for me, Eleanor." It was as though his command released some newly discovered spring and sent it unwinding in a glorious ribbon of sparks and colors.

"Merciful God…" This time when he covered her mouth, she took him, muffling her wild cry with his lips and tongue as he rode her through one orgasm into another. She used her nails, scoring his back again, relishing the feel of his flesh at her mercy.

He growled his pleasure, making her womb clench and begin another climb toward the pinnacle of release. Eleanor pressed her face against his chest to stifle her moans, tasting salty sweat and Mr. Burke.

"Wrap your legs around my hips." He thrust with quick, hard jabs that ended when his back became a taut, rigid line before he slumped over her. His whiskers scraped her neck eliciting a shiver, and though her body lay sated beneath his, her internal muscles twitched, gently caressing him.

"Good." His word was little more than a grunt, his voice—sandpaper rubbing her nerves.

Good? "Yes." She whispered the one word as his breath brushed her shoulder in ragged gusts.

She closed her eyes, seeking the strength to rise and leave his bed. She waited for him to say good night. He didn't. His labored breaths changed to snores. Understanding that as her cue to leave, she wiggled from under him and escaped.

Chapter Three

Eleanor gave up the idea of sleep. She crept to the bathing room and, using the mirror above the vanity, inspected her person. Horrified, she blinked in disbelief at her reflected image. Her hair, drenched and reeking of perspiration, was a sodden mess, and his salty sweat had dropped into her eyes, staining their color red. Worst of all, a bruise marked her neck where he'd nipped her.

The foundations of her life had trembled under Mr. Burke's impact. She wanted to huddle under a blanket and think. But she was afraid if she went to sleep she wouldn't wake up in time to cook breakfast.

Although it was the middle of the night, she bathed before dressing quietly and descending to the kitchen to begin the morning meal.

They say he makes a woman think Sunday is sin-day. Mable's words came back to her, reminding her she was only one among many who had graced her employer's mattress. *You think you can occupy my bed for six weeks and still look innocent?* His words mocked her after one encounter.

The smell of bread rising soothed her and she set to work, pinching off pieces of dough for clover rolls and pretending they were hunks of Mr. Burke's skin. *There will have to be rules. No public displays of carnal intent, no innuendo or rude glances, no touching when not engaged in night duty.*

The last consideration was important. The imprint of Mr. Burke's hands seemed branded on her rump. *I need to keep my wits about me and I can't when he's too close.*

Feeling somewhat better, she rolled and twisted more of the raw dough into strands, making cinnamon swirls before placing the full loaves in the oven to bake. Rather than repeat her earlier folly, Eleanor heaped rashers of bacon on platters, toasted bread and diced the potatoes she'd peeled the night before.

It was such plain fare and guilt for her skimpy night's offering still plagued her, she added a tray of crepes stuffed with melted cheese and thin strands of ham.

At the first sound of Mr. Burke's rising, she started scrambling eggs, sprinkling in green onions and adding crushed bacon to the mix. She was at home—in her element—in control. *The kitchen must be my domain.*

He came through the door and her self-confidence scampered back inside, hiding in a tight ball. He said nothing, crossing to stand behind her and peering at her morning preparations. She stepped toward the counter, turning to put the platter down so she could sneak a quick glance. He was clean shaven and looked better rested than Eleanor felt. He put his hand possessively on her hip.

"Good morning, Mr. Burke. As you can see, I'm working. I feel it would be better to keep our more familiar encounters for the night." She edged away from him.

His response was to reach over her shoulder, steal a slice of bacon with one hand and pat her bottom with the other. He surrounded her, forcing her to look back and up to continue her conversation. "Mr. Burke, this is my work area and—"

His mouth covered hers, cutting off her words. She held herself rigid until he released her. When he lifted his head, peering down into her eyes, she steadied her voice before saying firmly, "There must be a clean demarcation between day activities and night duty."

"Best get it on, I'm calling 'em in to eat." His manner was offhand, disinterested in her opinion, and he ate the piece of bacon, chewing on it as he stepped away.

She knew she was in hell when fifteen men in dirty boots trailed through the kitchen leaving straw, mud and horse manure in their wake. Eleanor divided her attention between the filth on the floor and her concern about how the men would receive her second meal in Mr. Burke's employment.

"Better." Her employer came to the kitchen in search of the coffeepot and approved her breakfast with one word confirming her early assessment. Mr. Burke was the quintessential male — insufferably arrogant.

Eleanor started mopping the floor. She scrubbed hard, removing the most recent layer of dirt before he held the kitchen door open, ready to lead the pack across her wet floor and out the back door.

"You can't come through. I'm cleaning." She faced him defiantly.

"Eleanor, you're not much more than five feet and a pinch and I've got you by at least a hundred pounds. You figure you can stop me with that mop?" His eyes, dark pools of wicked humor, challenged her to keep him out. But then he turned and spoke to the men over his shoulder.

"Use the front entrance from now on. No more traipsing through the kitchen. We don't want to rile the cook."

Mr. Burke came through the doorway himself though, took another cinnamon swirl from the extras stacked on a plate and leaned against the counter, watching her labor.

She'd been so close to him the night before she knew the exact pattern of his chest hair. The memory of being under him embarrassed Eleanor so much she couldn't look at his face. Her eyes remained on the mop but she couldn't stop the blush stealing from under her collar, staining her cheeks pink.

"If you wear a hole in the floor where you're scrubbin' so hard, I'll dock your pay," he drawled.

"Come here." His voice was so serious she glanced up, meeting his bland gaze. He brushed crumbs from his hands, straightened his big frame and gestured for her to come to him.

Reluctantly she set the mop in the bucket and crossed to where he waited.

"Never done work like this before, have you?" He picked up her hands, stripping her white work gloves away and studying the new red lines and the blister forming on her thumb in spite of the protection.

"No." Her response was clipped and sharp. Eleanor was certain his question covered all of her duties so far, although it was her current mopping he seemed to reference. "Any complaints?" He tipped her chin up, forcing her to meet his gaze.

Clamping her lips tight to keep from biting him, Eleanor shook her head.

"Cat got your tongue all the sudden, Eleanor?" He taunted her, daring her to whine about any of her duties.

"I have no complaints. Working as your housekeeper and collecting my wage is important, Mr. Burke—entertaining you with conversation isn't." Although rage simmered in her veins, she was proud of her steady reply.

"You taste as sweet as your treats." He caressed her cheek lightly before releasing her and grabbing a cookie on his way out, motioning her to follow him.

The compliment was unexpected and made her blush harder, remembering his lips murmuring against her neck.

"If you need help for any reason, bang on this and someone will come running." He pointed to the huge bell dangling on a long chain.

"I appreciate your consideration," she murmured her thanks, realizing from the former day how isolated and alone she'd be when the ranch crew went to work.

He shrugged aside her words and left.

Eleanor returned to the kitchen and finished mopping the floor. It was hard work, generating renewed appreciation for all of the servants who had kept William's house so immaculately. She owed her current survival to them.

"I didn't even get to say goodbye to the staff." The last day in the household, Mother Lacey had visited her early in the morning and informed her that she was being returned to the Alcotts. By the time Eleanor had reached the carriage, she'd been aware that something was terribly amiss.

Wilson, the Lacey's butler, had impassively helped her into the shuttered conveyance. Black curtains had been drawn, making her fear one of her family had died.

No explanations had been forthcoming. When she'd been driven to ask the Lacey employee for information, he'd helped her into the carriage, stammering over her address as he closed the door, "It is not for me to say. Godspeed, Mrs. Lac… Miss Al… m'lady."

Thank God my time in William's home wasn't a complete waste. She'd been so bored, she'd learned each domestic task, enabling her to guide the servants and better manage the household. Hence she was virtually trained for the employment she'd found — except in one area of course — she lacked mattress skills.

Mr. Burke has no concern other than his male satisfaction. She shuddered, trying to feel disgust, but arousal coursed through her as she relived the moment her body had spun out of control. *He made me feel things I've never experienced before.*

"I had no idea intimate relations could be enjoyable," she murmured in wonder. Her naïveté seemed as limitless as his knowledge.

Everything from Mr. Burke's nose to his toes overwhelmed her. Even his earthy, sweaty man smell drugged her senses when he was near. Her body felt as though it had somehow reinvented itself during the night, commanding her attentions in ways never thought of before. Her thighs ached, her ribs were tender and her sexual center felt strangely hollow, as though hungry to be filled again.

Grateful for the distraction the work afforded, Eleanor did the laundry, making a moue of distaste as she sorted through socks that needed darning, shirts without buttons and filthy denims.

Cyrus frowned thoughtfully as he walked toward the barn. He'd come awake when she'd wiggled out from under him the night before. Figuring she was going to use the water closet and come back, he'd disposed of the filled rubber and played possum waiting for her return. Left alone, he'd leisurely stroked his cock, planning on seconds. She'd crept past the bedroom door and he'd listened to the stairs creak as she descended.

It irritated him more in the light of day than it had last night. He saddled up and mounted, grinding his hard-on against the leather seat. Scowling, he gave the day's orders. The men were more interested in the status of the cook than in work.

"Hope you didn't scare her off, boss," Henley said.

"What'd she call them things wrapped around cheese and ham?" Jake asked, then added, "I could eat a plate of 'em every morning and nothin' else if you don't run her off."

"You hired her, right?" It was Hank this time, chiming in with his own concern.

"For God's sake, it's only food." He nudged his horse into a trot, swearing under his breath, but it wasn't her breakfast on his mind.

In the dark, she'd been silent under him, only her soft gasps and sweet musk signaling her readiness as her liquid heat eased his way through her velvet folds. He wore her scratches underneath his shirt and every time the fabric pulled tight, his cock remembered the feel of her nails digging into his back as he rode her.

But this morning she'd been Mrs. Prim 'n' Proper again, staring at him from her smoky purple eyes and delivering her suggested amendments to their agreement. He wanted to go back and bury himself between her thighs. Instead he concentrated on business—fencing.

It was late morning when he took a break. Jake sidled his horse close as Cyrus mopped sweat from his face. It was the housekeeper the foreman wanted to talk about, not the steers he was supposed to be rounding up.

"In case anyone asks, you put your duds in the bunkhouse when she took up residence in the house. Right?"

"She's a respectable woman. Make sure that's understood." Early on, Cyrus had made it standard procedure to protect a woman's reputation when she moved to the ranch. His ranch hands knew when to look the other way. If some of the women hadn't been so discreet, well, that was their own fool problem.

* * * * *

As Cyrus approached the ranch house at dusk, the smell of fresh-baked bread greeted him and even as his steps quickened—as did the steps of every one of his crew—he recognized the fleeting nature of the experience. Mrs. Lacey was temporary help, a fact everyone needed to remember. But goddamn, great food was awe-inspiring. Eager to experience his new cook's latest offering, he hustled to get to supper.

"Wipe your feet," he told the men, sending them to the front entrance as he headed for the back door. His lips twitched into a grin remembering the way Eleanor had faced him, mop in hand, protecting her territory earlier in the day.

After supper, the dining hall emptied and she cleared the table for him to work on his ranch ledger. He did more thinking about her than his notations, working with half his brain while he kept an ear cocked toward the kitchen. The meal had been fine, the men were enthralled with the cook, and if he wanted to get rid of her, he'd have a rebellion on his hands.

Every time he thought of her contentious stance on the bed the night before, arms crossed, hands fisted and ready for battle at the same time her nipples were waving at him, laughter rumbled in his chest.

"Eleanor, bring the coffee and come in here." Sounds had died down in the kitchen and Cyrus gave up work, ready for another round with Eleanor.

She came through the door carrying a plate of cookies, balancing two mugs in the crook of her arm with the pot in the other hand.

"Sit down. We have business to discuss." The cookies and coffee startled him. It had been some time since anyone had fixed a snack for him. His throat tightened, making his voice gruffer than he intended.

She paused by him, carefully setting the coffeepot down, followed by the plate of cookies. Then she placed a mug next to him, filled it and headed for the other end of the table.

"Stop," he ordered her.

She turned, her eyebrows signaling a question.

"Sit." He pointed at the chair next to him.

"If the next command is roll over, when do you want me to bark?" Eleanor's eyes took on a militant gleam.

"Dammit, sit down." *She's got her voice back.* His lips twitched in an almost smile.

"Yes, Mr. Burke." She returned to the chair next to him, pulling it out with mock humility.

"You're just itchin' to tell me off, aren't you?"

"Your poor excuse for manners calls it forth." She spoke firmly, her chin raising just enough to telegraph her superiority.

"You'll need to move whatever clothes you have into my room. I don't figure on chasing you down every time I want to fuck." He ignored her etiquette lesson and got right to the point. Last night's *one ride and I'm done attitude* wasn't going to work. He scowled at her, daring her to object.

"You want me to sleep with you in your bedroom—in your bed?" She shook her head, looking astonished.

"No, I planned on fixing you up with a pallet by the fireplace, chaining you there and having my way with you from time to time."

Cyrus studied her appalled expression, as if she believed he really might shackle her to the wall. Exasperated, he said, "Yes, I want you in my bed— all night."

"No." Her jaw was squared and there was no give in Mrs. Lacey's expression.

"Yes." Cyrus leaned closer, daring her to refuse again.

"Mr. Burke. Every servant is entitled to limited privacy. As a member of your staff, I am no different. I prefer to maintain my own living quarters."

"You sleep with me." He squinted at her, daring her to argue.

"I will report for night duty," she agreed in flat tones, holding his gaze stubbornly. "But I will leave when my work is completed. This point in our agreement is nonnegotiable."

"When I'm done, Eleanor, *if* you have the strength to crawl out of bed, have at it. But that means when *I'm* finished. Like I said, I don't plan on chasing you down every time I want between your thighs."

"You are crude but your message is understood. Of course, Mr. Burke." Martyred resignation coated her capitulation. She folded her hands on the table as though waiting for his next point of discussion.

"All night. In my bed. Whatever I want." The more she made it clear she wanted no part of sleeping with him, the more determined Cyrus was to make it so. And that graveled him since the other women coming and going could have slept in the barn for all he'd cared.

Her jaw was rigid and unspoken curses flashed from her eyes but she remained silent and from that, Cyrus knew Eleanor had something else on her mind.

He didn't relax or make the god-awful mistake of thinking he'd won. In little more than a day, Mrs. Lacey had invaded his kitchen, enthralled his crew, claimed his house and mesmerized his cock.

He bided his time, enjoying the show. Her cheeks were rosy from the heat of the kitchen making her eyes seem an even darker violet color. Wisps of blonde hair escaping the neat bun at her nape teased him.

"We need to discuss my contract with Mable." Eleanor tried to hold his gaze but he seemed more interested in her hair.

"I'm not interested. You have a deal with me. I own your time for six weeks. End of discussion." He picked up a cookie and ate it. "Take the pins out of your hair."

"I can do the baking here in the kitchen, in moments when I have spare time. It's only Wednesdays and Saturdays. Mable says she delivers on Wednesday and can pick up the desserts. You'll be going to town on Saturday and can carry them into her." Eleanor continued explaining her plan and was rewarded with his indifference.

She noted Mr. Burke's penchant for closing topics she wished to discuss and ignored his hairpin comment.

He reached behind her head and removed the tortoise shell comb holding her hair in place. Two pins later her sedate coif became heavy waves cascading down her back.

"If you have spare time, I'm paying you too much." He squinted at the strand between his fingers as if measuring its worth. "I'm not hauling cupcakes for you."

"All right." Eleanor braced for battle. Mr. Burke wore stubborn with pride. "I'm sorry we couldn't agree. It has been interesting working for you." Her hair slid from his grasp when she stood.

He growled, "What the hell is that supposed to mean? You cuttin' line one day into the contract?"

"My contract with Mable supersedes my deal with you." Eleanor started toward the stairs, despairingly sure she'd left herself no wiggle room. If he called her bluff, he'd be depositing her at the Mercantile's back door. Nevertheless, she made her voice firm when she said, "I'll get my things."

"Sit down and explain this agreement you have with Mable." He spoke curtly.

"I already did." Eleanor kept walking, reaching the base of the steps.

"Tell me again," Mr. Burke said sternly. "If you intend to go into business, learn to negotiate. You gave up too soon."

Eleanor disagreed. She felt rather euphoric and triumphant looking down at him as he found reasons for her to stay.

Cyrus had a sneaking suspicion he'd just been maneuvered. She wanted him to think her eager to leave and he wanted her to turn around and come back to her chair.

But she didn't. She climbed halfway up the stairs and then sat on a step looking down at him with her hands clasped before her.

Good negotiating strategy, make your opponent look up at you... He stood, which put them just about on eye level and she squirmed a little, having a hard time meeting his gaze.

"It's a matter of honor," she told him. Her words were sedate, calm. "Of course I would also like to further my bakery enterprise. But foremost, it seems important to fulfill the pledge I made."

"You promised to supply Mable with rolls and such twice a week, right?" Cyrus mulled it over, piecing together the strands of the conversation he'd ignored.

"No," she corrected him. "Just desserts. The order has grown quite impressively since we began our venture and Mable reports she's getting special requests if I have time to fill them."

"Then why move here?" he asked gruffly.

"I'm afraid I haven't been completely honest with you. I should have mentioned the reason I need a place to stay. After visiting very pleasantly with Uncle Henry and Aunt Millie for several months, circumstances in Hartford changed. Grandfather Alcott ordered me home and Uncle Henry insisted I obey."

"Anything else you forgot to mention?" Cyrus relaxed, getting comfortable in his stance as he watched Eleanor compose her answer. *Curiouser and curiouser... She's been in town for months and Henry didn't mention her.*

Nibbling her bottom lip, she assessed him and shifted uneasily on the hard step.

"You could come back down here and we'll both sit down to finish the talk."

She didn't move, remaining fixed to the step and staring at him.

"Why'd your late husband set you aside?"

"Who knows, really? We were childless, he wanted an heir. He formed a liaison with another woman. He wanted control of the Alcott-Lacey Bank..." She flinched, her answer piddling away.

"Didn't know the courts would let a man out of the noose on any of those grounds." Cyrus studied the pout of her lower lip waiting for her response. It wasn't long in coming. Her answer was clipped, her expression outraged.

"Four upright citizens, friends of William's, swore under oath they'd each conducted illicit affairs with me. They hadn't. I barely knew them. The divorce petition requested relief for reasons of adultery."

"Guess there was a dustup and your family shipped you here?" Cyrus scratched his jaw, thinking about swine who'd intentionally drag a lady through mud.

"After I publicly confronted one of the prevaricators, the gossip became even worse." Eleanor's angry expression changed to sad.

"You get in a good lick?" He hoped she had. It didn't sound like anyone else in the Alcott family had the stomach to do it.

"I wish, but—no. My aunt accompanied me to one of the miscreant's business offices. Afterward, William's friend swore that I'd begged him to recant his story. The conversation was just one more scandal the press seized and misrepresented."

"So let me see if I understand. If you're divorced, your deceased husband's estate belongs to someone else. If he dropped dead before the final decree, you get what's rightfully yours?"

"If it were only that simple. The Laceys are powerful members of Hartford society. Their family attorneys intentionally made William's accusations public, influencing popular opinion. They will not stop just because he's dead." Her words were bitter when she added, "Hindsight is a remarkable thing. It seems clear now that William had this planned prior to our wedding."

"Why in hell did you marry a snake like that in the first place? I took you for a better judge of character." Cyrus figured you could tell a lot about a woman by the man she hooked up with. He frowned at her doubtfully.

"Five years ago, during the 1883 financial panic, the Alcott Bank was in trouble. William invested with the stipulation that it become the Alcott-Lacey Bank of Hartford. Agreements were finalized making me Mrs. Lacey and William Vice President of Grandfather's bank. A stuffed doll could have been substituted in the ceremony." Eleanor's expression was grim.

"Your male relatives kill him?" Cyrus could see the way it had gone down. Eleanor had been security in a financial transaction. He tented his fingers, resting his chin on his thumbs.

"Of course nobody killed William. It's civilized in Hartford." She blinked, giving him a disgusted look.

"Sure sounds like it," Cyrus snorted. It didn't sound very civilized to him. "You certain he's dead?"

"Yes. William couldn't even die quietly. Last month, during a court hearing, he was taken with a fit of apoplexy." Her tone was disgusted. "No doubt the Lacey family would have hidden his death if they could. But he succumbed in the courtroom. By the evening newspapers, the tabloids were already titillating the public with the question of whether William and I were divorced. Grandfather telegraphed Uncle Henry the initial news before sending the newspaper account in the mail."

"And they want you home to settle up accounts and claim what's yours?" Cyrus could see why Eleanor was a tad put out. He looked at her with renewed interest. The widow was scrambling for purchase amidst upheaval. Interesting.

"Even if the courts decide I'm truly his widow, it doesn't matter. In Hartford I'll be remembered by society as William's barren, adulterous, cast-aside wife." She brushed her hair back from her face and said defiantly, "I'm not returning."

"Anyone seeing to the liars?" Cyrus decided he wouldn't mind killing a couple of the bastards for her.

"I have no idea what progress has been made in exposing their treachery," she admitted. "According to Uncle Henry, now that William is dead, so is the divorce. Grandfather's attorney has petitioned the courts to drop the case. The current expectation is that I will return to Hartford and fight with the Laceys over inheritance issues."

"So you're hiding here until they catch up with you and make you go back?"

"No, I have a plan." Her eyes sparkled and she inched her bottom down a step, leaning toward him with enthusiasm.

"I'm working here to earn start-up money for my shop." And then, realizing that she'd revealed her need for the housekeeping job, she scowled and said tartly, "If my current employment ends precipitously, I'll find other means. But my plans do not include Hartford."

He walked to the bottom of the stairs, squatted on his heels and looked up at her. It was a posture he used to lure a recalcitrant mare to the halter. He figured it was worth trying on a skittish housekeeper.

"This business you've started," he asked gruffly, "are you earning any money? Is it worth your time? Did you make a good deal or did Mable see how green you are and tie you up in a bargain where she makes all the profit and you do all the work?"

"We shook hands on our agreement."

"Well, is it a good deal?"

"Mable is an honest woman." She lowered herself another step.

"That's not what I asked." He stood, walked back to the table to pour a cup of coffee and sat down.

"Have you done your figures? Do you know how much each of these costs to make?" Sipping the lukewarm bitterness, he chased it with a bite of pecan sandy, waving the half-eaten cookie in the air before consuming it.

"Mable gave me the start-up ingredients and deducted their cost from the confections she sold. Then we split the profit." She came down the steps, sat on the chair next to him.

"You payin' wholesale or retail for the ingredients?"

"I don't know. I assumed... I don't know." She considered his question slowly, her brow puckering into a frown.

"And how will you use this money you're earning?" Cyrus reined her back in the direction he wanted to go.

"When you pay my wages at the end of six weeks, and I add in the money I make from my mercantile contract, I'll be able to rent that little empty building I mentioned before."

"What makes you think you'll have enough money then? Shoot, Eleanor, you've never even asked how much I'm paying you."

Cyrus didn't tell her he owned the flimsy shack she was dreaming about. Hell, it would probably get flattened by a good wind before Eleanor raised enough money to rent it.

Lavender eyes darkened to purple as she sputtered, "Of course I'll earn enough for all this work I'm doing." She demanded, "Won't I?"

Cyrus squirmed inside and his voice came out gruff when he finally answered.

"Business is business. If you're planning on making your livelihood from a store, you'd better know how much you're spending on your ingredients." He suddenly didn't want to douse the hope shining in her eyes, so slid past the building topic and centered on the one at hand.

"I'll do the arithmetic." She nodded eagerly.

"You might be better buying the fixins from Mable wholesale before you set your price next time."

"Oh I don't set the prices." She frowned. "Should I?"

"I'm not saying Mable Smyth isn't an honest woman. Hell, I've known her since I was a boy — she's as straight as an Indian lodge pole. But she's not above lettin' a fool be a fool."

"But we're both making money," Eleanor protested.

"She's making a sight more than you if she's charging you retail for her ingredients. Besides, you're doin' all the work." Cyrus pointed out the obvious.

"Even if I make nothing, the introduction of my pastries to the marketplace has given me an enormous start. I prefer to think that neither Mable nor I are fools." Her jaw squared, she flushed pink and her expression became militant.

"Maybe not." He conceded the point to her, pouring the last tepid drops of coffee into his cup. Actually he kind of liked the way she refused to let him undermine her loyalty to Mable.

"I'll put on a fresh pot." She took the cup from his hand, heading for the other room.

He followed her to the kitchen and leaned on the doorsill while she fiddled with the coffee and set it brewing. "You count in that cost?" He pointed his finger at the stove.

"What do you mean?"

"I mean, you don't own a stove and without mine you can't make squat. And did I hear you right? You're counting on me being your distributor, carrying your wares to the store and your ingredients back?"

"How much will that cost me?"

"How much can you afford?"

"I don't know." Her tone was exasperated.

"Well, figure it out," he told her. "If you want to run a business, you have to watch every cent coming and going."

He crossed to the stove, lifting the half-perked coffee from the fire.

"It's not done." Eleanor reached to pull it back in place.

"Time for bed."

"But I have things…" she began.

"Mable's already cuttin' into my Wednesdays and Saturdays." Cyrus acknowledged his defeat, claiming the important victory. "She's sure as hell not gettin' my nights. Upstairs, move your clothes and come to bed."

He turned and strode from the kitchen, willing her to follow. He wanted her so bad his gut ached. He was halfway to the steps when her tart answer floated from the kitchen.

"I will report for night duty shortly, Mr. Burke."

Chapter Four

Trying to compose her rioting emotions, Eleanor rubbed butter on the tops of the loaves and set them to rise. When her preparations were finished and she had no more excuses to linger, she trudged up the steps, flutters of anticipation mixed with confusion.

After denying her the right to honor her contract with Mable, Mr. Burke had shifted mid-discussion to picking apart her business plan. Apparently he had acquiesced and now waited above for her arrival so he could deliver his next work-related demand.

The move to his bedroom was silly. *I'll humor him until he goes to sleep, then return to my room as I always intended.*

Since she had few items to move, it took very little time to carry her satchel to the other room. Rebelliously, she left her dress behind.

"Come in here, Eleanor." As though he'd been listening to her progress, as soon as she'd deposited the satchel next to a chair, he called to her.

It was unheard of—venture into the bathing room while he used the facilities? She pretended not to hear. The next call was too loud to ignore. She crossed the hallway, cracking the door to peek inside.

"What?" she asked, staring at the wall instead of the man in the tub. One quick glance had been enough to confirm her fears. He was naked, expecting her to join him in the room to complete some nonsensical task he'd demand.

"Quit staring at the wall, come over here and wash my back." He made his outrageous suggestion in the voice of a general ordering his troops.

Nervously, Eleanor's gaze flicked sideways and he pounced, capturing her glance. He motioned her toward him, flipping water on the floor.

"You'll ruin the wood." She concentrated on the splatter of water instead of him.

"Throw a rug down and it'll be fine," he answered.

To do that, she'd have to move closer to his person—his unclothed body—his naked skin covered with nothing more than transparent water. She swallowed her fear and slowly crossed to where he sat in the water waiting.

"Is this part of night duty?" she asked.

"Yep," he drawled. Then gave her a sly look and asked, "You ever wash your old man's back?"

"You mean my father? Of course not. My father had his own manservant to attend his personal needs."

"Not your pa. Your dead husband. They tell me a good wife bathes her man."

Eleanor blinked at him, confused. She was the daughter of a prestigious Eastern family. She had to remind herself that she was also Mr. Burke's servant. *Cyrus wants me to wash his back? I can't think of him as Mr. Burke while I put my hands on his naked skin.*

Her intimate address would have to remain purely mental if she intended to maintain their employer and employee relationship. *I will think of him as Cyrus and call him Mr. Burke.* That settled, she answered him.

"No, Mr. Burke. My husband and I did not share such intimacies." She repressed a shudder remembering William's pudgy frame.

"Guess I'll have to teach you how then," Cyrus drawled. "Take this and lather it up good, then scrub my shoulders and back with it."

Eleanor accepted the dripping sponge and obediently rubbed it against the soap, coating it with lather.

"Okay, you've got the first part down," he growled sarcastically. "There's foam dropping on the floor you're so worried about. Now let's see if you can manage the next step."

"You'll have to lean forward." Eleanor knelt at the end of the tub, sponge in hand. Her breath caught when she saw the scratch marks she'd left the night before. They were reminders of their coupling and her limbs felt weak anticipating another encounter.

"I can't believe I'm doing this," she muttered to cover her heated response.

"I should charge you for your instructions." Of course he heard and taunted back.

Eleanor squeezed the sponge full of water over his head, sending a cascade of frothy liquid over his face.

"Why in hell did you do that?" he sputtered.

"I didn't have a bucket of water to use," she answered grimly.

Eleanor decided washing his back was the safest way to avoid whatever else he had planned. She trickled water in a stream downward, enjoying the way his muscles twitched and he jerked under the tickling caress.

"Your tongue would feel good doin' the same," he suggested.

"Why would I want to lick your back?" Eleanor asked, startled at the way the idea made her sex clench.

"You don't want to taste me?" he asked innocently.

"No," she lied, remembering the flavor of his sweat.

"Not even a nibble?" He ignored her rebuff, reaching around to grasp her skirt, tugging on it.

"Let go of my dress," she snapped.

"Might be better if you shucked it altogether before you climb in here."

"You want me to disrobe and get in the tub with you?" *The man has lost his mind.*

"Yep. There's nothing like sharing a bath with a woman to get to know her better."

"Good night, Mr. Burke. Your back is clean. Your suggestion is impertinent and we know each other quite well enough. I'll leave you to finish your ablutions alone." Eleanor's face flamed and she stood, throwing the sponge at his head before hurrying to the door.

"Eleanor, I didn't give you permission to leave." The sound of water splashing on the floor accompanied his warning as his wet feet hit the floor.

She slammed shut the door and took off running, making it down the stairs and outside to the swing with him following close behind.

"Eleanor, you sure you want to conduct our business out here?" He came out on the porch, his nakedness outlined by the house light.

She edged behind the swing, keeping it between them. Speechless, she gazed at the beast stalking her. His bare feet were big, his long legs topped by muscled thighs and the evidence of his manhood jutted rigidly in front of him as if it were made of steel.

Gauging the distance to the steps leading to the ranch yard, Eleanor risked a glance away from the savage.

"You run off the porch and I'm gonna chase you," he drawled, crossing his arms over his chest. Waiting for her next move, he added, "Might be kind of fun."

"Don't you have something better to do than tormenting me?" she asked tartly.

"Yep, I figured on doing it in that bed upstairs. But if it's the porch you've decided on, I'm flexible."

"If you'll put on some clothes, I'll come back into the house." Eleanor drew in a deep breath waiting for him to agree—then she'd get off the porch and run like hell toward the big gate and the town beyond.

"Nope, no point in it," he said. "They'd be comin' back off as soon as you hit the door."

"Your brains were addled by a head injury, right?" Cornered and unconvinced she could persuade her cowboy boss to come to his senses, she gripped the railing, ready to sprint for the steps.

"Eleanor, did I not agree to haul your desserts to town?" If he hadn't been stark naked it would have been a reasonable question.

"I don't know what you agreed to. Worse yet, I don't know what I agreed to," she muttered, inching her way closer to her goal.

"Did I not tell you my housekeepers had night duty too?" he growled.

"You didn't say night duty included cavorting naked in a bathtub with you," Eleanor answered swiftly.

"You haven't done much playing in your life, have you, Eleanor?" he asked. Then seeing her glance toward the steps again he said sternly, "Don't move. I'll be right back."

As soon as he went through the door, she studied her escape to nowhere, hesitating before she started her descent.

"Eleanor." His voice cracked out like a whip drawing her gaze to where he stood draped in a blanket that covered him from neck to knees. "Sit down in the swing. We'll negotiate some."

Dreading the coming conversation, she took a seat. As soon as her feet left the porch floor, he walked to where she sat in the swing, unfurled his blanket, wrapped it around both of them, and slid next to her, pulling her tight against his bare thigh.

Eleanor gasped, jerking in shock when Cyrus reached down and untangled her clenched hands, laying the right one on his bare leg.

"Just settle down. All we're doin' is talking a bit." He covered her fingers, capturing her hand between his warm palm and warmer thigh, sending heat scorching through her. Lazily he propelled the swing into motion, his left arm embracing her shoulders, her body hugging his.

"Eleanor, the way I see it, we made a deal and finalized it last night. If you didn't agree to the terms, you shouldn't have accepted the contract."

Before she could protest further, he dropped his head and nuzzled her neck.

"Did you not enjoy yourself?" he whispered the question in her ear.

"I'd rather not speak about it." She averted her gaze, staring at the barn.

He moved his hand, pulling hers with it in a slide through the fine hair on his thigh. Her fingers clenched, grabbing his skin in a pinching hold, preventing the upward climb.

"You brand me, I put my mark on you in the same place." His low chuckle brushed across her ear, his breath warming her as he leaned closer with his promise.

She released her grip.

"Burns where you touched me," he drawled. Then, instead of rubbing his own leg, he dropped his left arm to her side and put his hand on her thigh, mirroring the spot she'd pinched.

"Right about here," he said, stroking her limb, his heat radiating through her skirts.

"What do you want from me?" she asked desperately.

"Well, aside from two meals a day, a clean house and you warming my bed, I wouldn't mind you dropping the Mr. Burke and calling me Cyrus."

Since she'd just been arguing with herself about the same thing, her answer was already framed. "Mr. Burke, I'm your temporary housekeeper. Using your given name would signify we have a relationship other than employee and employer." She closed her eyes and sighed, holding her head rigid where it lay against his shoulder.

"Not interested in anything else, huh?"

"What? Resident doxy, slattern with a mop? Of course I'm not interested in anything else." She grabbed his arm, stopping the hand on her thigh from moving higher. "I have to maintain a reputation above reproach in order to be tolerated in town when I set up my shop. It will be hard enough keeping my presence here on your ranch a secret. Flaunting an illicit relationship is unthinkable."

"Your reputation is safe with me, Eleanor. Mable knew that when she sent you out here."

Cyrus shrugged and sent the swing gliding back and forth again.

Since his fingers had resumed their slow crawl, towing her hand toward his shaft, Eleanor didn't find his reassurance convincing.

"We're sitting here in a porch swing, you're totally nude under this blanket and the men in the bunkhouse can surely see your intentions are not honorable." She wasn't stupid, just hopeful somehow the men would remain quiet.

"You don't need to worry about them talking. My men have sense enough to keep their gobs shut. If there's gossip it won't start here." He squeezed her thigh and slid his hand upward again.

"I expect Aunt Mildred will be instrumental in spreading the news if she finds out I'm here." Eleanor turned her head and unintentionally rubbed her cheek against his chest. His warmth against her face made her want to purr. Instead she quelled the urge and sat up straighter.

"Nope, that's not going to happen either," Cyrus told her. "That would be Henry's wife, right?"

"Yes," Eleanor agreed. "But during my visit with them it was clear Aunt Mildred loved gossiping. I don't think she can resist." She didn't tell him that Aunt Millie's favorite topic was him.

"Henry's not likely to want his dirty laundry aired in public." Cyrus made a disgusted noise, pulling her tighter into his embrace.

"Uncle Henry is henpecked and Mildred doesn't listen," Eleanor explained.

"She understands she likes to eat and they'll be out on the street if she runs her mouth." Cyrus interrupted.

"Why?" Eleanor craned her head backward, trying to see his face in the dark.

"Why do you think Mable sent you here?"

"Well, because I needed a job and a place to stay." Eleanor started to explain again.

"Nope," he said. "Because Mable knows when Henry can't stifle his wife, I can."

"How?"

"I own the bank." Cyrus said calmly.

"You are in banking, like Grandfather?" Was this yet another manipulation on the part of her family to conduct a business transaction? Eleanor froze.

"Nope," he drawled. "I just don't trust others to manage my money so I built my own, got a state charter and set up a bank close to home. I hired your uncle away from the bank in Paris."

Eleanor didn't know whether to warn him or not. It was common knowledge in the family that Uncle Henry had been sent to Texas to expand the family's banking interests.

Cyrus' laughter rumbled under her ear, changing the direction of her thoughts.

"You're enjoying this. Aren't you?"

"Yep."

His callous enjoyment of her ordeal made her stiffen, wiggling to get free from his embrace. Her inclination to caution him evaporated. *If the Alcotts gobble you up, so be it, Mr. Cyrus Burke.*

"The way I see it," he drawled, "you're a respectable woman who fell from grace while doing right. Now you're reclaiming your place in society by doing wrong with me. If you consider it that way, it all seems pretty damn laughable." He pulled her back down, adjusting her body against his side, her head again resting on his chest. "You worry too much, Ellie.

"Eleanor," she corrected him.

"Ellie, we've got six weeks to have some fun and I'm all for enjoying your stay while you're here." His fingers stroked her thigh, leaving a trail of heat there. His soft laughter brushed across her senses.

"Bet I can make you scream again." He smoothed the folds of her dress, his caress lighting a torch in the flesh beneath.

"You are shameless." Eleanor flushed with embarrassment at his reference to their coupling the previous night. She'd been unable to stifle her cries during one incredible orgasm.

"Yep," he agreed. "Never found much use for shame. I'm more into tasting," he murmured in her ear before he nibbled her earlobe. "And smelling," he brushed his nose against her hair, rubbing his face in the strands, inhaling the scent, "and touching." He shifted her slightly, covering her hand again.

Eleanor shivered, another wave of heat flushing her skin as he lifted her hand and cupped it around his engorged shaft. He made soothing noises in his throat, sounds that became a low hum of pleasure as he guided her fingers up and down, stroking the hard length she palmed.

It was so hot inside the blanket at first she didn't realize he'd lifted her skirt. She shivered as the heat from his hand painted a blush of desire up her thigh. When his fingers brushed through her nether curls, she whimpered.

"You give in to temptation often, Eleanor?" he asked.

"Never," she answered honestly.

"That's too bad, Ellie," he murmured. "Everyone needs a pinch of naughty from time to time."

Abruptly Cyrus stood, pulling the blanket tighter around both of them, leading her toward the ranch door.

"Where are we going?"

"To bed," he growled, moving Eleanor through the door and toward the upstairs.

Cyrus ushered her up the steps, listening to her fuss at him along the way.

"I have to prepare rolls for breakfast." She tried to veer off to the kitchen.

"Later."

"Do you always get your own way?"

"Yep," he told her. "And right now my way is upstairs in bed." His cock had already turned to stone as he hurried her along. "Eleanor, this isn't a good time to debate my management style."

In the bedroom, he made short work of her clothes, rendering her naked before he led her to the bed. Standing her in front of him, he sat on the edge of the mattress, ready to roll on a condom.

Cyrus prided himself on his ability to go long and hard, drawing bed sports out for hours before spilling his seed. But as he looked at Eleanor, every muscle in his body tensed. The need to shoot squeezed his nuts like a vise.

"Turn the light off—please." The first part was a crisp demand. She added the last, softening it to a polite request as she stared at the wall above his head.

If she'd whimpered, he'd've let her have her way. But there she was, ready to do battle again. *So we're going to pretend you don't want it tonight, huh?*

Cyrus relaxed inch by inch, regaining his control as his sense of humor kicked in. God in heaven, he could smell her arousal, her skin was flushed with desire and her nipples stood at attention, begging to be sucked.

"Nope." He smiled when he refused her. "I want to watch us fucking tonight."

"You are a sinful devil." Apparently scandalized, her gaze unlocked from the wall and shifted to his face.

"Yep," Cyrus said and grinned. "Now that we're clear on my character, you can put this on." He handed her the condom.

He pulled her closer to him until she stood between his legs. Her lips parted in astonishment as her creamy skin blossomed pink. Eleanor, of the cult of pure womanhood, held the rubber in her hand and peered down at his cock.

"I-I-I… I don't know how," she stuttered.

"Think of my dick as a tool you're covering." Swear to God, he felt as long and thick as her rolling pin when he growled his instructions.

Eleanor caught her lower lip in her teeth, biting on it as she prepared to sheathe him. He brought her hand to his engorged member, wrapping her palm around his naked length before he leaned back on the mattress, thrusting upward in her grasp. "Familiarize yourself with my equipment, Eleanor."

He kept her hand wrapped in his because she looked mutinous, ready to argue.

"This is unnecessary. You are an idiot." She squeezed his shaft for emphasis.

He couldn't control his grunt of pleasure.

Startled, she squeezed him again and said, "Your eyes look strange."

No doubt they were crossed and about to roll back in his head. He released his grip when she tentatively began to explore on her own. Her fingers reached the liquid seeping from his slit and she jerked away, stroking down his bare length once before coming back to investigate his pre-cum. When she swirled her finger around his cock head and peered closer, his jaw locked tight and his toes curled.

"Cover. My. Tool," he managed to say.

She did, biting her lower lip again and frowning as though performing an arduous chore. By the time she'd rolled on the rubber and smoothed it twice, he was rigid.

"There, it's done." She sighed and straightened between his legs.

"Straddle me." His cock, covered and ready, waved in the air. Cyrus parted Eleanor's thighs and pushed his knees between them.

"It looks dangerous," she muttered, staring down at the thick rod he intended to impale her with. "I don't want to."

"Yes you do," Cyrus advised her, positioning her the way he wanted in spite of her protests.

Eleanor remained stiff, parting her legs around his thighs, straining to remain above his cock, but the lips of her sex brushed against the end, teasing both of them.

"Put it in," he growled, desperate to sink into her slick heat.

Cyrus gazed at Ellie's breasts on level with his mouth then leisurely tasted one nipple, sucking on it before he switched to the other.

"Juicy, plump, sweet," he told her. He rolled the peak on his tongue, biting down on the tip, enjoying her look of shocked pleasure as he cradled her rump, directing her downward descent. "Come and get me."

"You are a wicked, wicked man," Eleanor gasped and then moaned, clutching his ears and pulling his head up so she could smash her lips against his.

Since Eleanor didn't have a clue about the way of kissing, Cyrus took charge, nudging through her velvet walls at the same time he tongue-danced with her above.

His breath came in labored gasps accompanying Ellie's moans when he released her mouth. He guided her up and down on his shaft, her honey making her greased and slick.

"Swivel your hips, Ellie." He pressed his thumb against her pearl and she ground against it, releasing more liquid, drenching her folds.

"Mr. Burke," she whispered, eyes unfocused and smoky purple.

"Feels good, doesn't it, Ellie?" He wanted to give her as good as he got, and by damn what she had between her legs was fine and special. He took away his thumb and brought her tight against his groin.

"Rock forward." He showed her how to thrust her pearl against his flesh, satisfying both of them.

Ellie had a way of moaning that made him want to lie back and let her fuck him all night long. Her rump clenched, her inner muscles contracted around his cock, and waves of goose bumps washed over her skin as her release jolted through her.

"Keep it going, baby," he told her, riding her orgasm and pushing her into another. Her channel flexed, tightening her walls and creating friction as he nudged her breast in place and mouthed her nipple before sucking on the tip. A roar built in his chest, as if he were an animal trying to unleash a bellow. He stifled it, pumping her up and down on his cock, drawing her release out and doubling his pleasure.

Not ready to finish, he pulled out of her and repositioned her on her knees. Spreading her thighs wider, he rubbed his cock in her wet folds, drawing her liquid from pearl to anal rosette. She shuddered and flinched when he touched her virgin hole.

"Absolutely not," she gasped.

"Another day," he promised, brushing his knob against the tight pucker before moving back to her creamy folds. Leaning over her shoulder, he pressed her head down on her arms and slid his hand under her belly, lifting her rump high for him.

Her ass was rosy red and he leaned close, nipping one cheek than the other before parting the lips of her sex with his cock and sinking into her vulnerable flesh with one hard thrust.

"Goddamn that's good," he groaned, looking into dazed eyes as she stared over her shoulder at him. He pushed her hair aside so he could see her expression better as he fucked her. "Watch," he ordered her.

Her emissions coated his cock, making it easy to piston hard and fast. Each thrust went deeper. He pushed her legs wider, hauling her ass higher at the same time he growled, "Don't look away."

She obeyed, her lips falling open, her panted breaths mingling with his groans. Jesus God, he couldn't get enough of her. He pulled her to the edge of the bed and growled, "Now give it to me again. Come for me, baby, while I ride you home."

She pressed her face into the covers, stifling her cries as he pumped into her from behind, rubbing the nubbin of nerves at her apex until she shattered.

When he ran his thumb down her crack and stroked her rosebud, her channel clenched tighter, her orgasm pulsing and milking his dick.

Cyrus released, spilling into the tight material gloving him, only regretting that he wasn't shooting his seed into the sweet woman he rode.

"Damned if you don't pull it out of a man, Ellie." His hips moved in short, hard, jarring thrusts before he collapsed sideways and groaned.

Eventually he stripped off the rubber, threw it in the can by the bed, pulled a sheet over Eleanor, doused the light and curled around her ready to sleep. He was almost under when he felt her inching toward the edge of the mattress. His hand snaked out and caught her arm.

"Stay put," he told her. "I'll want seconds soon."

"Impossible," she groaned. "I have to rest."

"Guess your old man wasn't good for more than one a night, huh?" Cyrus could think of a lot more things he wanted to do before he slept.

"Fifty-four," she mumbled.

Chapter Five

"Fifty-four what?" The number hung there in the air between them until he couldn't stand it any longer. "What kind of marathon are you claiming?"

"We had marital relations fifty-four times."

"Must have been a hell of a party."

"During our marriage, over the five years we were wed, we had relations fifty-four times — once a month, until the last six months — when we had none." She suddenly wasn't too tired to set him straight as she clarified using precise words.

He rolled over, fumbled with the light, and stared at her. Eleanor's hands were plucking the sheet nervously.

Cyrus remained silent, trying to figure out why in the hell Eleanor's man hadn't been fucking her senseless three times a day — morning, noon and all night—like he planned to. When he said nothing, she went on.

"We slept in separate bedrooms. I never saw him unclothed. Never. Decent men and women don't comport themselves in carnal behavior."

"Is that right?" he drawled. "What if a man isn't decently inclined?"

"It is a married woman's duty to keep her husband on a righteous path. I failed." Prim and proper to the last, she repeated what she knew as fact.

"If that be the case, I'm glad I've escaped the noose." Cyrus blew out the light and curled around her again. "I can assure you, your man didn't find anything better than you. Now go to sleep." Her breathing became less agitated, gradually matching his as he rubbed his face against her hair and spooned around her.

He'd already figured out that his widowed housekeeper had less experience than most second-day brides. His uneasy feelings were tempered with smug satisfaction. *Guess I'll have to teach her how to please a man.*

The second time they coupled during the night left them both panting and exhausted. Under cover of darkness, Eleanor lost the rest of her inhibitions, writhing under him, matching her rhythm to his and holding on when the going got rough.

When Cyrus came, collapsing with a groan, he patted her hip and rolled to his side of the bed.

"Good night, Mr. Burke." Eleanor turned her back and pulled the sheet over her.

He woke to find the sun creeping into view, turning dark to morning light. He had Eleanor's head cradled on his chest, her hand splayed open on his thigh two inches from his dick. Lazily he contemplated waking her for thirds, but before he could, her eyes popped open, meeting his gaze alertly.

"It's late," she said, scrambling to leave the bed. "I've got dough I didn't punch down last night." She grabbed her nightgown and hurried on her way. "Breakfast can't be late."

He groaned and rolled over, pulling the pillow over his head. As usual, Eleanor had the last word. She'd left him sporting a morning hard-on with no place to put it.

He was hungry for more than breakfast when the men filed into the dining hall. Apparently oblivious to him, Eleanor moved quietly around the table, filling the men's coffee cups, switching out platters of food, and generally tending her business and ignoring his. His morning cock stand re-engorged when Eleanor stretched over the table, refilling a plate of toast. He savored the sausage drenched in syrup at the same time he savagely forked flapjacks, contemplating firing his cook for dereliction of duty.

Eleanor left and his cock had just begun to settle down when Henley finished off the last pancake.

"You need to marry someone like that, boss. It would be a nice thing to have good eats like this year-round," he muttered, his mouth full.

"Jesus fucking Christ," Cyrus snarled. "She's fed you three days and you're ready to sell my freedom for a goddamned flapjack. Henley, ride drag today and eat dust."

The men didn't linger over coffee after that and Cyrus followed them toward the door, irritated at Eleanor for being a good cook.

"Mr. Burke, might I have a moment of your time?" Before he could escape, she stopped him.

"Not now." He tried to brush past her and keep moving. Slapping his hat against his leg as much to hide his erection as to vent irritation, he headed for the door. Walking was already painful and riding the ridge of his hard-on all day was going to be pure torture.

"Mr. Burke, I need a word with you." She put her hand on his arm, tugging him to a stop. It was impossible for her to look down her nose at him, since he was a foot and a half taller, but she sure as hell tried.

"I said I'd haul your tomfoolery into town. We don't have anything else to say. I'll deduct the cost from your wages." He shrugged his arm, trying to shake her hand free.

"I need to tell you something," she said, hanging on.

"Eleanor," he warned her. "You need to step away." She was so close the sweet perfume of her musk swamped him and his nuts turned to stone.

"I heard what that ranch hand suggested and I knew immediately that, arrogant as you are, you would decide I'm attempting to trap you into a marriage." Her chin elevated and her eyes flashed scorn when she said, "I just want to make it perfectly clear that is not the case. You are safe from my wiles. I will never marry again."

"Of course you will." Cyrus snorted and shook his arm, trying to shed her touch.

"Want us to go on without you, Cyrus?" His foreman took that moment to ride up to the porch and shout.

"I'm on my way," he yelled back, scowling at Eleanor.

"Whether you think I'm plotting to snare you or not, lovely as they are, your continued attentions hold no allure for me. Kindly remember in your pin-brain that I am working to earn money for my pastry shop." Eleanor's words were tart and for his ears alone.

Cyrus' cock jumped as he watched her nibble her bottom lip as if tasting him again and he backed toward the door before he lost control and pounced on her. She followed.

"Eleanor, me and my pin-brain have work to do. The boys are waiting." All the blood in his body surged south, his breath constricting so tightly the words came out in a rough parody of his usual voice.

"Of course. I'm sorry for keeping you, Mr. Burke." She backed up, putting distance between them, her expressive eyes snapping fire.

He was halfway down the steps and another surge of lust stopped him in his tracks. Turning around, he went back inside. She'd moved to the table, clearing up the remnants of the morning meal. He crossed the room, stepping behind her as she reached for a platter.

"What now?" She looked over her shoulder irritably.

Fitting his groin against her rump, he reached around her, pressing his hand to her flat stomach, urging her backward against his denim-covered arousal.

"If it's collecting wages you're after, it's not going to happen if you keep calling me names and I fire you." Then he leaned over her shoulder and murmured in her ear. "Leave off the drawers this afternoon. I might have time to sample some of your fine dessert when I come through."

His cock still ached and his belly burned, but irritation had changed to humor and he had to tamp down the laughter rumbling in his chest. *Might have time, my ass...*

He spent the morning stringing wire around a fouled waterhole, his mood undimmed by the extra

106

work. Images of his thick knob working its way through her snug sheath flitted through his head. *No wonder she's tight. Hell, she's barely broke to ride.* More than once, he had to suppress a groan.

The thought of her bare-assed naked under her dress and ready for him made him clench the barbed wire so tight, he had to take off his leather glove and untangle it. His scruples about bedding a respectable woman were disappearing as fast as Eleanor's desserts at mealtime.

She called me a pin-brain for thinking she'd want marriage. Her "I'll never marry again" left him more disgruntled than it should have. *Of course she'll marry again. Hell, I'm doing her a service letting her see how good it could be — with someone else,* he amended.

His grim expression changed to a satisfied grin. *She said it was lovely.* Then he thought of Henley's ill-timed words at breakfast. *"It would be a nice thing to have good eats like this year-round."*

"Yep," Cyrus muttered aloud.

* * * * *

"Oh my," Eleanor whispered, giggling nervously like she never had when she was a schoolgirl. Feeling decadent and sinful, she crept to the bedroom and removed her pantalettes. When she returned downstairs, thinking about the tepid couplings she'd experienced with her late husband,

Eleanor picked up a scone, buttered it and took a bite.

The sweet nutty mixture erased the memory of William, reminding her of Cyrus instead. He'd carried the flavor of her pecan sandy on his lips when she'd kissed him the night before. It had been a spontaneous action. She'd...

Eleanor closed her eyes and rolled the honey mixture on her tongue. *He tasted like ambrosia.* Then she snorted at her own thoughts.

"He tasted like coffee, cookies and, and..." Her words stuttered to a stop. He'd licked the walls of her mouth, his teeth biting her tongue as he'd sucked on it.

Remembering, her nipples pebbled, her womb clenched, her breath caught and ripples of desire coursed through her. Carefully Eleanor laid the half-eaten scone on the counter, brushing her hands free of crumbs and picking up a basket of darning before going outside.

She sat in the porch swing, cool air stirring against her bare legs hidden under her dress. The motion of the swing vaguely reminded her of their rhythmic coupling. He'd been insatiable and unrelenting.

"That's it, Ellie," he'd growled. "Play with me a little bit. I've got a ways to go yet."

Play with me... In her world devoted to duty, there had been very little play. She'd married a man who furthered her grandfather's business interests, she'd been ignored in her husband's home and cast aside and hidden by both families when her use was at end.

There seemed little reason to deny herself this pleasure. She'd had more fun in two days than in the rest of her life. The work was challenging but appreciated. Her boss was arrogant and completely mesmerizing. It also appeared that night duty was his dessert for each day. *I have six weeks during which to enjoy this pinch of naughty Cyrus prescribed.*

She frowned. Night duty had seemed manageable when he'd included it in the job description. But Cyrus Burke wasn't manageable.

The swing rocked back and forth as Eleanor concentrated on finding a button to match the others on his shirt.

"He owns a bank." Unease filled her. He'd said he'd hired Uncle Henry away from the bank in Paris, Texas. Eleanor knew perfectly well that Henry Alcott didn't go anywhere Grandfather didn't send him. So if Uncle Henry worked for Cyrus, it was because the Alcott Banking Company was interested in his bank.

Cyrus had been smugly confident that he could control his employee. Eleanor wasn't nearly as certain. Minus her pantalettes and waiting for his return, her thoughts flitted between stewing over whether she should warn the arrogant fool and savoring the previous night's astonishing events.

When Cyrus and two other men rode into the ranch yard, Eleanor took her mending inside and watched the barn from the kitchen window. Her sex clenched in panicked anticipation as he strode through the back door.

"Stay right where you are and hang on." He was moving fast and giving orders as he joined her in front of the sink, placing her hands on the counter.

"You want me to stare out the window?" She looked at him over her shoulder, following his directive to grasp the ledge.

"Nope," he answered, pulling one of the gold devices from his back pocket and deftly rolling it over his member. "You hold on to the counter and steady yourself. I'll watch for cowboys who might take a mind to roust me out."

Before she understood his intentions, he stepped behind her, flipping her skirts up to her waist, holding them in place between their bodies.

"Mr. Burke," she squeaked, once again shocked by his actions.

He ignored her protest, sliding a hand to the juncture of her legs, parting the lips of her sex. She shuddered and he grunted a monosyllabic sound that might have been "Good."

Eleanor's breath huffed out in excited pants as he positioned himself at her entrance.

"Are you ready, Ellie?"

"The pantry." She was mortified and aroused at the same time. As he teased her pearl, she moaned, "Oh God."

"Told the boys I wouldn't be long. Better enjoy yourself while you can," he whispered in her ear, making her insides quiver.

"Have you lost your mind? This is barbaric, we could be discovered, it's totally decadent..." Heat flooded her body and liquid flowed from her core.

"Eleanor, hush." He shushed her words by covering her lips with his. Pressing his groin against her buttocks, he tilted her hips enough to match their sexes. She winced when he thrust through her tight passage, still tender from the night before. He stopped.

Eleanor tightened the walls of her channel, demanding he continue. He growled, a low rumble escaping his chest. Reaching around to find her nubbin of pleasure, he stroked it with skill. His touch sent intoxicating pleasure rippling through her.

"This is wicked." Urgently she jerked her mouth from his, gasping for breath.

"Yep," he agreed, shoving her corset down and cupping her breast, caressing the rounded globe before closing finger and thumb to pull and pinch her nipple.

"I didn't play enough with these last night." As if to show her what she'd missed, he twisted the stiff peak, making Eleanor jerk, thrusting her breast against the caress.

She couldn't remain still, sinuously rolling her hips as her walls gripped his shaft in a tight squeeze. Her breath was a tight rattle in her throat as sensations threatened to smother her.

"I'm going to eat you up tonight." He brought her to the edge of release and whispered in her ear, "Jesus God, you're sweet and tight." Cyrus thrust deeper, rubbing his groin against her rump before withdrawing to thrust again.

"If you don't stop," she panted, "I'm going to scream."

He answered her challenge by pulling his shaft all the way out, teasing both of them. Her gasp of dismay was a soft begging sound.

"When you scream, I'll stop. Might want to muffle it some, I see Bill heading this way."

"Please," she implored Cyrus. Blurry-eyed, Eleanor stared out the window, sighting the man who approached the ranch house.

"Yep," the heathen reprobate agreed. "That's what I aim to do—please you." He took that moment to plunge into her again, pinching her pearl at the same time he pulled on her nipple.

She shattered in a swirl of delicious pulsing heat, her wild cry caught by the arm he provided as her shriek forced its way from her lips. He came in short hard jerks she felt all the way to her womb.

Dizzy and weak, she slumped against the sink. He petted her lower curls, dropped her skirts and stripped off the condom as she stared panic-stricken out the window. The cowboy she'd seen walking toward the house hesitated, looking at the closer back entrance before veering off, striding toward the front.

In a moment, the sound of the door opening accompanied the cowboy's words. "You 'bout ready to head out, boss?"

"Just washing my hands," Cyrus answered. "Go ahead and mount up. I'm coming."

Eleanor walked on trembling legs to the table. He disposed of the rubber device he'd filled, adjusted his pants and followed behind, patting her rump before she collapsed on a chair.

"Don't let me keep you from your work." He handed her the basket of darning.

Apparently he was unfazed by the event. It was quite some time before Eleanor's hands were steady enough to thread the needle. Sternly she told herself she would have to speak to him about the line separating day and night duties.

In order to keep her wits about her, she needed time away from him to take care of housekeeping tasks and focus on her future. But when once again she sat in the swing sewing on his buttons, her skin burned remembering his touch, her womb clenched hungrily and the sound of her embarrassed laughter escaped into the summer day.

Cyrus thought his knees might buckle before he made it to the barn. Good God he'd come like a sonovabitch. Warnings went off in his head. His new housekeeper had only been here a few days and he was ready to break all his rules. First he'd pulled her into his bed full-time and now he was slacking off, hanging around for afternoon dessert.

"Lovely or not, I'll just have to explain to her she can only have it at night." He muttered his intentions aloud.

He didn't get the chance to set her straight. As usual, Eleanor tried to take charge. After supper was cleared, he poured a glass of whiskey and prepared for a discussion. She entered from the kitchen, wiping her hands on her apron and beat him to it.

"It is inappropriate to couple in the hours of daylight. Besides, I, for one, have work that needs attention and I've no extra time for dallying."

"Guess I'll have to catch you between jobs. Leave the bloomers off. You never know when my baser instincts will require some more dallying." In spite of his earlier decision, he couldn't let her get the last word.

She opened her mouth to sass and he said, "You got any on now?"

"I've got work to finish, pastries to prepare, bread to work." Her face turned beet red and she backed toward the kitchen.

"Best get at it then and leave off telling me how to manage my help." He sipped his whiskey and grinned, enjoying her flustered retreat.

* * * * *

Cyrus spent the better part of every night that week exploring wickedness with the widow. By Friday he was so damned tired, he got careless. He was stringing barbed wire, thinking about his trip to Board Town, the red-light district in Paris, and almost stepped on a rattler. Then, like a fool, he nearly shot himself in the foot when he killed it.

It jarred sense into him. His mind was on fun and not business. Many a man had lost it all by such careless inattention. The next morning, Cyrus dropped off Eleanor's pastries at Mable's store and then made the trip to Paris. He had business to take care of before he could concentrate on fun.

He visited his lawyer while he was there, the one who'd investigated Henry Alcott before Cyrus made him bank president. After he gave Lawyer Jud another assignment and sent a telegram to Sage Beckett, Cyrus went shopping at Molly's Interesting Incidentals. Molly was a whore with good business sense. At the back of her dress shop in Board Town she also ran a sex shop. He picked up his condoms and went back to the telegraph office and retrieved Sage's return message. *Arriving Monday.*

He'd considered it from every angle and knew his decision was sound. Never mind that he'd only known her a week, Eleanor would make a fine permanent housekeeper. As soon as he made sure her story was on the up-and-up, he'd offer her steady employment. *Hell, I'm solving all her problems and mine too.*

* * * * *

By the end of the first week, Eleanor found it quite intoxicating running a household to suit herself. Her initial reserve began crumbling.

"Thank you, ma'am. Those were fine eats." The cowboys were polite, wiping their feet on the way in, taking their hats off at the door, shuffling to the table for meals and complimenting her by cleaning their plates.

Cyrus though, was underfoot much more frequently. On the Monday of her second week of employment, he brought a new ranch hand to the house and introduced him.

"Eleanor, this is Sage Beckett. He's going to be ramrodding the outside work while I concentrate on inside business for a while. He eats plenty so better add another measure to your fixings." Then he turned to the new man and grinned. "Sage, when you taste Ellie's meals, you'll thank me for calling you here."

Mr. Beckett gave her an appraising look and from the interaction between the two men she felt certain he was Cyrus' friend, not just another employee.

Sage did eat a lot and after his first bite of her sweet potato pie, he'd aimed a look her way and drawled, "They say the way to a man's heart is through his belly. I'm in love, Mrs. Lacey. Marry me."

The men ringing the table laughed and chimed in their own declarations.

"You go marrying her off, boys, and that'll be the end of the chocolate éclairs." Cyrus stopped the laughter with his sarcastic opinion. After that, the men concentrated on their food and quit their teasing remarks.

On Wednesday, she started working on the oak planking in the dining hall, scrubbing it, sanding it in spots, and polishing it to a mellow shine. At supper, the ranch hands respectfully wiped their feet before they entered, acknowledging her efforts.

"I have the other half to complete tomorrow," she told them, pride in her voice. Cyrus might be assured of the discretion of his employees but she was certain the men stood ready to hold her in contempt as another of his doxies if she gave them reason.

She concentrated on the household tasks, hoping her labors would earn their esteem and if they spoke of her later, they'd mention the floors, not the porch swing.

There was nothing respectful at all about Mr. Burke, though. The next day, he lingered in the house, coming out of his office from time to time to watch her work.

Eleanor's limbs ached from crawling and her knees were chafed. She was not in the mood for any of his nonsense and ignored him accordingly. Little by little she became uncomfortably aware of her derriere in the air and the way his glance seemed fixed on it. She attempted to stand, but the inflexibility of her corset turned it into an awkward scramble.

The corset was stiff, an uncomfortable binding, pinching her painfully when she tried to bend or reach. She wore it as part of her kit, her armor she donned every day to face the world.

"Leave the corset off from now on. Hell, you can't breathe in that device. Next thing you know you'll suffocate and then I'll be out a cook." He crossed the room and pulled her to her feet, poking his finger against her dress and then running his hands down to her waist.

"A respectable woman doesn't present herself publicly without proper undergarments, Mr. Burke. Not even a cook," she told him sedately.

Cyrus shrugged, saying no more about it, and when he left the house, she forgot about the corset, assuming he had too.

Silly her. Eleanor quickly understood that Cyrus didn't forget anything. He just sidled back to a subject in unexpected ways.

Chapter Six

Eleanor creaked along in the kitchen, moving like an old woman. All day, as she'd crawled over the floor finishing her task, she'd been planning a before-bed luxury. She'd waited until Cyrus became engrossed in his after-supper accounts before quietly climbing to the bathing room.

She drew a bath and quickly began disrobing, intending to be in bed and asleep before he came upstairs. Wrong. She'd removed her dress and started on her corset when the door opened. She froze.

"I'm going to bathe," she said lamely.

"I see that." Carrying a bottle of spirits and an empty glass, he set them down next to the tub, leaned against the wall and, crossing his arms, inspected her.

"I'll hurry," she told him. The vexation that flickered constantly when he was near began to simmer. Her planned leisurely soak was interrupted. Eleanor pointed at the door. "You can leave now."

Instead, he pushed away from the wall and pounced on her, deftly unhooking the corset and peeling it off. Red marks marred the underside of her breasts and bruised pinches showed even through her thin chemise.

"That's history. Don't wear it again." He threw the corset on the floor.

She was in the process of explaining to him that she'd wear ten corsets layered on top of each other if she chose when she realized he wasn't paying any attention to her words. He was staring at the juncture of her legs clearly outlined through the thin material of her last garment.

"You trim your lower hair?" he asked.

"What?" Her face flamed and she slapped her hands over the part of her anatomy he leered at. "You are totally reprehensible. Leave."

"Nope. Since you're not into sharin', I'll just wait here and get in line for the tub."

"You are not going to watch me bathe." But there was no getting him out of the room so finally she stepped into the tub still wearing her chemise, ducking under the water before removing the thin garment.

"Hell, I've seen it all already. What are you so shy about?"

"Yes, you have," she agreed crossly. "So stop looking and let me have this moment in peace." Eleanor closed her eyes, hoping he'd go away if she gave him no encouragement. She should have known better. Recognizing the sound of his clothes hitting the floor, she wasn't surprised when his foot brushed hers as he stepped into the other end of the tub. She opened her eyes in time to see his big frame slide into the water.

Pulling her knees up to her chin, Eleanor glared at him. She could see that she'd lost her comforting soak. Angry words were on her lips when he grinned and slapped the surface of the water, sending a splash up to drench her face.

"Your behavior is childish." But she found it hard to lecture a man without looking at him and since she'd caught a glimpse of his shaft standing tall in the water, she focused on the wall instead.

Eleanor tried to avoid touching him, but he sprawled, claiming every inch of space she'd abandoned.

"Relax, Ellie. Unfold your legs. Hell, it's a big tub. There's room for both of us." Stretching his legs out, first he rested a big foot on either side of her. When her knees remained folded, he hooked a foot under one, pulling until she obeyed. She no sooner slid her feet forward than he grabbed them, putting a foot on each of his thighs.

"See, that's better than all scrunched up the way you were."

If she closed her eyes and listened to him, she'd swear he was interested only in her comfort. Cyrus had a way of wrapping seduction in innocent-sounding sincerity.

She peeked through her lashes, assessing the situation. There wasn't much room and what there was, he claimed. Before long, he used his feet to catch her hips, inching her forward enough until his heels hooked behind her. His pretense of platonic bathing had ended.

"Would you leave me alone?"

"Nope." Cyrus pulled on her rump, moving her toward him as her legs slid higher, riding his hips instead of his thighs.

"Lean on back, Ellie, let's just soak a little and talk." He groaned, rolling his shoulders against the end of the tub, his eyes closed.

"I don't want to talk," she muttered. But she did want to soak. She eased her shoulders against her end of the tub, sinking lower in the warm water, letting the washcloth float to the surface and hide parts of her anatomy.

It was hard to believe that in less than two weeks, she'd gone from arguing with him on the porch to sharing a bath with the man. His ability to manipulate and seduce was rather extraordinary. She studied him, looking for signs of her own exhaustion and found none. He was lean and fit, working every day as if he were a machine.

His features—large nose, stubborn jaw and sun-and-frown-lines crossing his broad forehead—made his face too craggy to be called handsome. And when his eyes were open, his gaze was too direct, commanding her attention. She almost snickered when she looked at his prominent beak. And good Lord, he poked it in her business without shame.

Though his words were often crude and always nosy, she liked talking to him. It was invigorating, like a jousting match. She sighed. In other circumstances, Cyrus would have made a good friend. He really did seem benign just then, relaxed and resting with his eyes—and mouth—shut. She leaned back and closed her lids, not opening them even when she heard the clink of bottle against glass.

"Taste this and see what you think?" He waved the glass under her nose, inviting her to sip.

"Fennel." she murmured, keeping her eyes shut. "I can't remember whether it's a flowering herb or a root. Our gardener grew both it and anise. I believe it's good for indigestion." She waved it away without looking at him. "No, thank you. "

"It's called absinthe, and it's damned expensive spirits. Now taste."

"Yes, I'm familiar with the flavor. I've used a pinch of anise to flavor my spiced almond biscotti on occasion." Eleanor obediently accepted the glass, sipped, rolled the liquid on her tongue, swallowed and sipped again before handing it back.

"Is that right?" he drawled, tipping the glass for a drink before handing it back to her. When she would have declined, he distracted her with a question. "Are your knees sore?"

"When I finish soaking, they'll be fine." She flexed them tentatively.

"The floor'll just get messed up again. You've got the boys trained to come through the front door now." Instead of offering some kind of balm for her tender joints, he pointed out the futility of her actions.

"You need to buy a rug." Eleanor closed her eyes again, contemplating smacking him over the head.

"Throw an old worn-out towel down." Cyrus splashed water at her, rippling the water in the tub.

"And cover part of that magnificent oak floor under a rag?" Eleanor sat up straight looking at him indignantly. It was an opportunity to take him to task about other things. "The fireplace is as grand as any I've seen, yet you've allowed the handsome flagstone to become marred with soot. Your windows have no curtains to frame the beautiful view. And though the walls of this house are solid, weather has chipped away the paint. Mr. Burke, you insult the builder by your lack of care."

"Is that right?" he drawled, taking the glass from her, emptying the contents in a gulp before filling it again.

"Buy — a — rug." She leaned closer, her nipples brushing the top of the water as she ordered him.

"I built the house." He handed her the glass.

"Oh." Covering her surprise, she sipped absinthe, meditating on this information before saying tartly, "Well, take better care of it."

"That's what I pay you to do," he drawled and took the glass back.

"Buy a rug," she repeated and hid behind closed lids, sliding lower, suddenly aware of her breasts bobbing in the water as she argued with him.

Cutting off her retreat, he angled his big foot, sweeping her forward as if he were a croupier raking in his winnings. Without opening her eyes, Eleanor gripped the sides of the tub, stopping her forward motion.

"You like my house?" His question was designed to distract her and it did.

"Very much," she told him, opening her eyes. "It seems settled, as if it's been here a long time. When did you build it?" He'd balanced the glass on the edge of the tub and she picked it up, admiring the bathing room.

"Started on it the year I bought the land. Didn't get it finished for another two or three — hell, it's not really finished now. I'm restin' between ideas." He lay in the water, feigning exhaustion.

"Well, your home is quite lovely now that I'm uncovering its treasures. You did well, Mr. Burke." Eleanor complimented him before taking another sip of liquor and handing it to him. The water lapped against her, gently surrounding her in an oasis of calm. She closed her eyes again, floating placidly in nirvana.

"Your turn to answer a question," Cyrus said as he filled the glass again. "What was your home like, with all the gardeners and servants? Miss it?"

"That's three questions," she corrected him, waving her finger at him for emphasis before answering his inquiry. "Number one—Grandfather's home is a tomb of quietude. Nobody speaks above a whisper and all the servants are afraid of him. Number two—his gardens are magnificent but no better squash or cuke was ever grown than what I've found in your patch. Number three—yes, I miss my sisters and my aunt."

"What happened to your ma and pa?"

She felt her bottom lip quiver and Eleanor reached for the glass of absinthe, not waiting for Cyrus to hand it to her. "Dead, long ago," she said flatly. "Had I not left Hartford, my sisters would also have been dead as far as society was concerned." She looked at the drink and then downed it, blinking tears from her lashes.

Shuddering, she inhaled deeply, remembering her last morning with them. They'd waited to hear her destination, vowing to join her where ever she was sent. It had been bravado, and they'd all known it.

"When I'm established... " When she had her business operating successfully she would invite them. Biting her lower lip, she thought of the shack next to Mable's store, not exactly a promising home.

"Tell me about when you were a little girl. How did you spend your days?"

"What do you mean?" Eleanor frowned, remembering her childhood and Grandfather's rules. "Most of the time we had to be verrry quiet." She drew the word out, picturing the four of them underfoot in the cook's kitchen, avoiding the old man who'd taken them in.

"Phoebe is a scholar. Augusta is a wunderkind with mechanical devices and Josephine is an artist. "

"So Phoebe read a book, Augusta tinkered with the cookstove and Josephine drew everyone's picture. What did you do?"

She closed her eyes again and smiled. "The cook let me make desserts."

"Sounds like pretty tame goings-on," Cyrus chuckled.

"Noise was discouraged," Eleanor mumbled defensively. Then a childhood dream popped into her thoughts and she smiled at him, ready to share. "I wanted to run away and join the circus."

Cyrus snorted. "Let me guess. You were going to sell baked goods and make a fortune."

"No." she mumbled, feeling drowsy and content. She waved her finger back and forth making an arc.

"What then?"

She pried her eyes open and answered. "I wanted to swing on a trapeze and fly through the air high above everyone on the ground."

He moved his feet, drawing her closer again, and she could either slide under the water or let him guide her to her destination. The night was so mellow and she didn't feel like arguing so she complied, finding herself pulled up on his lap until she straddled his thighs.

"Your grandpa take you to the circus?" Cyrus asked her.

She hiccupped. "Good Lord, no. Grandfather was horrified and there was 'hell and damnation' being shouted after our Aunt Tia escorted us home and we confessed where we'd been."

He laughed and she looked up at him, trying to remember what she'd been talking about. Oh yes, family.

"And you?" she asked, stroking the dark whiskers on his jaw, preparing to rest her head on his chest and go to sleep. "Do you have relatives? It's a big house. Why did you build it?" She yawned sleepily.

"I built it for my mama," he drawled. "She died before I got it finished."

"That's so sad. I'm sure she's proud of you as she watches from above." Eleanor squinted up at the ceiling trying to picture Cyrus' mother viewing him from heaven then back at him, lolling in the tub. "Well, maybe she's not looking right now."

Flustered at the idea of angelic eyes witnessing the scene, she decided it was time to depart the tub.

"I'm all wrinkled." Eleanor thrust her hand in front of his eyes, dripping water on his nose, showing him. She didn't want to be impolite, but she really had been in the water a long time. She grasped his shoulders, levering herself upward, preparing to climb from the tub.

"You ever get to fly like you wanted?" Cyrus slid his hands up her hips and caught hold of her, lodging his cock against her belly, trapping his shaft between their bodies as he brushed his lips across hers in a kiss.

"Only recently. At night. With you." Eleanor heard a silly giggle and realized the sound had escaped from her. "Oh," she looked at him. "I feel rather giddy." She hiccupped and held her breath.

There she was, drunker than a Saturday night cowboy, weaving and dancing over his cock, tempting him to sink it deep and forget about putting cover between him and sure-fire disaster. He had a policy. He never fucked bareback. He just didn't. But goddamn it right then he wanted to. She was cute as a button, with her uninhibited bouncing and giggles. He wanted to wrap her in his arms and love on her all night with nothing standing between them.

Instead he made her stand up, still straddling his thighs so her mound was on eye-level with him. She giggled again, a sound so foreign from her usual prim notes he had to look up and check her eyes to see if she was still lucid. She was and she wasn't. Instead of giving him her usual glare, she winked.

"I trim it," she said.

He looked back at the short hairs feathering along the seam of her cleft and blew a puff of air on the lips of her sex. "Why?" he asked curiously.

"It's more subdued," she said sedately and folded her arms, watching him inspect her. "Well, did I clip it too short?"

"See if you can hook your leg over my shoulder. I want to look a little closer to see what kind of job you did."

"I can't do that," Eleanor shook her head. "Water is sure to splash all over the floor." She tapped him on the nose, scolding him.

"I'll sop it up with a towel." Before she could argue more, he lifted her leg, resting her thigh on his shoulder.

"Like that?" She shifted unsteadily on her one leg, trying to get comfortable.

He didn't answer. His stuck out his tongue and licked.

"That tickled." She grabbed his head and laughed. "Do it again."

She was cocked open and ready for him and he buried his face, bumping his nose against her nub of pleasure at the same time he explored her entrance. He flicked in and out, feeling the mouth of her channel squeeze shut trying to catch his tongue. Holding her by the rump, he pulled her closer and commenced eating her up.

He didn't have to tell her what to do. Her hips did a slow roll, grinding into the sensation. Damn, she tasted fine. Hot honey flowed for him and he savored it, sliding his tongue as deep as he could, using his nose to rub her pearl.

When she came, she latched on to his ears for purchase, muffling the sound of her scream as her orgasm rolled over her. But damn, what he could hear sounded good — she moaned begging for more even as he kissed and tasted her back to earth.

Gently he shifted her leg, letting her slide back into the water before he sat up on his knees facing her. His cock jutted out, about even with her head and she looked at it, bleary-eyed but game.

"My turn," she said and stuck her tongue out, licking the white cream already dribbling from his slit. She closed her eyes and did one of those taste-testing things. He could see her concentrating on the flavor as she rolled it around in her mouth. He held his breath, cursing himself for forgetting to have a condom ready to slap on.

Women didn't suck naked dicks. At least none he'd ever had wanted to actually put their mouth on him. Which was fine. A hot mouth on a rubber-coated cock was almost as good as a tight pussy.

"Delicious." She licked her lips and went back for another swipe.

"Suck on it," he growled, forgetting about the condom, cupping her face and presenting more of *delicious*.

She did. By God, she wrapped her lips around the head of his cock and sucked hard enough to pull his stones through his nose. "Easy there," he cautioned, not wanting her to stop but not sure she wouldn't decide to take a bite in a moment.

"It has an odd texture," she said before taking him deeper, the end of his cock brushing the back of her throat. She tilted her head, trying to talk while she explored, commenting in garbled speech as she ran her tongue over, around and then down his shaft.

She gagged and he tensed, ready to pull out and apologize. She grabbed him by the ass, pulled him closer, and hollowed her cheeks, sucking him deeper with long pulls that spelled his imminent demise.

Cyrus let her play until the last possible moment but before he came in her mouth and made her sick, he thought he'd better back off a bit. She slapped his hands when he tried to pry her mouth off him.

"Goddamn, don't say I didn't try," he groaned and lost it, pumping in and out of her mouth and watching her swallow his seed as it jetted out of him. With back bowed and muscles rigid, his orgasm blasted through him like hellfire and he knew it was the best goddamn fucking he'd ever had.

He got both of them out of the tub before they collapsed and drowned in the three inches of water left in the bottom. Kicking a towel over the spill on the floor, he carried her to the bedroom.

"That was lovely, just lovely," she said, rubbing her head against his chest.

"Yep," he agreed. He didn't even consider ruining the night with a rubber glove corrupting the sensations. He pulled her on top of him, arranged her thighs over his face and her face over his cock, and they did it again—and again.

When she started to flag, he fucked her with one finger, then two, sucking her pearl and licking her honey while she writhed on top of him and did the same for him, laving his cock with her mouth and tongue, swallowing it deep. And when he came, damned if Ellie didn't drink his release as though it were French champagne.

Cyrus pulled her up beside him, resting his chin on her head. She pressed her face against his chest and snored softly. He didn't think he was drunk, but his world was rocking sideways just the same.

It wasn't hard playing a sophisticated lover with a woman as inexperienced as Ellie. Hell, she made him feel like a stud. Possessively, he tightened his arms around her. *Pastry shop be damned, Ellie isn't leaving.*

* * * * *

Cyrus woke with a smile on his face, picturing Ellie on a trapeze. The night before, she'd been wild, uninhibited and flying with the greatest of ease. His satisfied grin changed to a frown.

She was drunk. He should feel guilty for plying her with alcohol. He didn't. Cyrus was pretty damned sure that as soon as Eleanor woke, she'd point out the error of his ways. He kept his eyes clamped shut, enjoying his memories, not ready to face feminine hysterics or accusations.

She twitched next to him and then he could feel her creeping toward the side of the mattress. Cyrus turned his head and met her gaze. Her eyes, smoky lavender and as big as fifty-cent pieces, blinked at him and he knew — she remembered.

She scrambled off the bed, grabbed the sheet to hide her nakedness and headed for the door. He cleared his throat, preparing to say something even if it was wrong.

At the sound, Eleanor turned, facing him, her blonde hair tumbling around her shoulders and pink flesh peeping out of the sheet. She was a wet dream come alive. As they stared at each other, her cheeks blushed rosy and her eyes deepened to purple.

She held a finger up. "Not a word."

She ordered his silence, he agreed it was a good time to keep his mouth shut, and she left, presumably to get dressed but more likely to hide.

Cyrus pulled on his own clothes, trying to get his wits about him. Since she hadn't run screaming from the bedroom or tendered her resignation, he took that as agreement that their night had been mighty fine. As he was tucking in his shirt, he remembered the corset.

He couldn't resist deviling her some more so he put on his most autocratic expression and followed her to the bathing room. Sure as hell, she was trying to sneak it on before he arrived. His tension melted into laughter he was hard put not to show.

"Leave it off," he ordered her.

"I told you that would happen." In the process of hooking the corset, Eleanor paused, pointing at the water marking the floor.

Cyrus snorted, recognizing misdirection and avoidance. Pulling her into his arms, he rocked her against his big frame, hugging her close.

"You taste delicious too." Tipping her chin up, Cyrus brushed his lips across Ellie's, trying to keep from whooping laughter at the blush threatening to incinerate her. Patting her on the fanny he added, "Better get breakfast started, sweetheart. I'll take care of this."

She fled.

He mopped up the mess, giving the room a final satisfied look before glancing up at the ceiling. Remembering Ellie's concern about a heavenly witness, he flinched. *Mama, if you're watching over me from up there, you need to close your eyes for a spell.*

Chapter Seven

By the end of her second week of employment, Eleanor realized she'd formed a tendre for her boss. When he was gone, she composed sassy remarks she'd say to him. When he was with her, whether it was a quick visit in the afternoon or a long sensuous night in his bed, every beat of her heart was attuned to what he said and did. She found ways to spoil him—trimming his hair, rubbing linseed oil into his work glove to make it supple and soft, and even polishing his boots.

Eleanor was besotted, enjoying the freedom of working alone in the house, choosing which task to undertake or set aside as her mood dictated. She found housekeeping for the dear man arduous but wonderfully satisfying. He was a rustic rascal, endearing under his gruff exterior.

Their harmonious relationship had her daydreaming like a fifteen-year-old girl over her first sweetheart. She reveled in the home she was creating for him and in her zeal, moved her cleaning and primping to the second floor — to the closet in his bedroom to be exact.

Her sentimental thoughts and maudlin affection screeched to a halt when she uncovered a purple garter sporting a garish red rose, followed by an assortment of silk stockings, a lush green velvet robe, corset strings and a pair of mauve slippers.

"I wonder if William bought his lady love such items." Eleanor stared at the castoffs from a long line of predecessors. Nothing could have reminded her so eloquently of her status. Rubbing the velvet material between her fingers, she inspected the wares — expensive, flamboyant and wicked. She snooped further, looking with interest at the sheer scarves she found tucked in a wooden chest. The box also held a supply of condoms plentiful enough to provide for the needs of an army battalion.

She was appalled. Scandalized. The tenets of decent womanhood resounded in her head. She was furious.

"Thank God I found these before I made a bigger fool of myself." She vibrated indignation at the same time it occurred to her that she was now as much a floozy as William's mistress.

* * * * *

Two evenings later, Eleanor had already retired for the night but returned to the kitchen for a last chore. She hurried downstairs, not bothering to light a lamp while she fiddled with her breakfast preparations. Cyrus was outside tending his garden, talking over ranch business with his friend, Sage Beckett.

"You planning on telling me why you called me here?" Beckett asked.

Eleanor wondered the same thing. Beckett's sudden appearance did seem odd given that there was already a foreman on the ranch.

"I brought you here to watch over the spread while I do my courting." Cyrus straightened, passing one bucket to be refilled and picking up the other. "I've been looking for a permanent solution to my housekeeping problems for a long time. Never thought I'd say it, but I intend to take a wife. Mrs. Lacey fits all my requirements and then some."

Happiness blossomed in Eleanor's heart and she smiled, her previous animus melting away. So she *was* more than just one of the many women who'd graced his sheets.

Sage snorted. "Thought you'd be protecting your territory after the boys started considering your housekeeper's marriage prospects. Why this woman? If I recall, it was you who said all cats look the same in the dark."

Ready to march outside and use a skillet to clobber Sage Beckett over the head, Eleanor waited

141

for Cyrus to put the other man in his place. Instead, he laughed.

"But not all cats can cook," Cyrus said smugly.

"You've only known her —"

"Around two weeks," Cyrus interrupted. "And that's long enough to recognize a good deal when I see it. Damn, Sage. Do you have any idea how much time and trouble, not to mention money I'll save by marrying Ellie?"

"You scoundrel," she murmured.

"There's hidden costs dealing with females, old friend," Sage reminded him, laughing as he walked away.

Indeed. Eleanor itemized those costs as she slipped into bed, waiting for Cyrus to join her.

* * * * *

A few days later, Cyrus stood inspecting the changes in his house. The cobwebs were gone from the corners and he was exhausted, testimony to Eleanor's recent whirlwind activity both downstairs and up. At night, she fucked him until his brains rattled in his head. During the day — frowning, he crossed to look out the clean window — more evidence of her labor. He should have been pleased. Instead he felt uneasy, as though he'd missed something.

Sage stuck his head in the front door, interrupting Cyrus with ranch business. "Your mare's restless. She may foal before morning."

"I'll check on her during the night."

"You don't need me. Admit it. You brought me here to appreciate your find." Sage pointedly glanced at the kitchen where they could hear Ellie moving around.

"Maybe," Cyrus said gruffly. "Anyway, I have to scope out the situation before I begin my negotiations. No sense in offering more than necessary to get it done." He shut up his negotiating talk when Eleanor entered the hall carrying a tray loaded with pastries.

"I thought you might share these with the ranch crew. After they sample them for me, they might be able to suggest what will sell the best."

As Sage reached for the tray, Eleanor smiled brightly at him. Cyrus felt a prickle of jealously run up his spine. He said stiffly, "Don't be spoiling my ranch hands."

"We'll let you know what we think." Sage winked, whisking the tray from Ellie and balancing it in one hand as he ate an éclair on his way to the bunkhouse.

"You're serious about this pastry business, aren't you?" Cyrus admired anyone with grit and Eleanor had her share, but her plans were getting in the way of his.

"Yes. Mable says my building needs a new roof."

He opened his mouth to let her know she didn't need the building or the roof. She had his—permanently. But she wanted to talk pastry shop and wore a distant expression not conducive to proposals. *Probably been working too hard. I owe her extra for cobweb removal.*

"Mable says the owner refuses to make improvements."

"Give me a list of what you want done, and I'll pass it on. A month should be plenty of time to get it ready."

"I'll need a sign for my business. And don't forget the shelves that should be no more than shoulder high, and of course, the counter top—"

"I'll tell the owner." Cyrus interrupted her. Dammit she had her list of needs ready at hand.

"Why thank you, Mr. Burke. I appreciate your help. Mable suggested the owner is sometimes difficult in business matters." She hesitated on her way upstairs. "My pastries are ready for tomorrow…"

"Your desserts will continue to get transported—as we arranged." *So Mable says I'm disagreeable. I'll need to have a word with the old lady. Does she think I'm the kind of bastard who'd cheat Ellie?*

Cyrus didn't want to be classified with the sorry bunch who'd taken advantage of Eleanor. Then he squirmed remembering the night he'd plied her with liquor. *A decent woman like that left to the mercy of a man like me.* Half of him was appalled at Eleanor's unfair fall from grace. The other half was damned glad he'd been around to catch her.

After she went to bed, he visited the kitchen and inspected the confections packed loosely, each new row separated by tissue paper layered in boxes.

"Pretty fancy fare for a town like ours." Selling baked goods seemed like a silly plan for Eleanor to make a living. "Good thing I don't intend to cut her loose."

Eleanor found her employer's pragmatic plan to lure her into unpaid servitude outrageous. Rather than become either his slave or a castoff memento gracing his closet floor, she'd decided to demonstrate her value, making a dent in both his wallet and his hard head on the way out the door. Sighing, she stepped into the tub, organizing her strategies as she relaxed. She woke when Cyrus lifted her from the water.

"Jesus Christ, girl, it's a wonder you didn't drown in here."

Before she could protest or thoroughly come awake, he tucked her into bed and slid in behind her, wrapping her in his heat. "Don't pay attention to me. Just go back to sleep."

She kept her eyes closed when he nibbled her ear, sending heat coursing through her veins. He lifted her thigh, entering her with gentle thrusts from behind, and her muscles clenched, tightening her cunny around his shaft. He grunted his appreciation, burying himself deeper, splaying her butt cheeks wider.

"Feels good, doesn't it, Ellie? How about you?" Cyrus cupped her breast, tweaking the nipple while below he stroked his hard length in and out of her.

"Yes," she groaned, turning her head to whisper her agreement against his lips. His hand burned hot—a brand of fire across her stomach. Suddenly, he lifted her, positioning her on her knees, her head pillowed on her arms, her rump in the air.

"Feel," he ordered her. And she did, squeezing his shaft and relaxing then tightening again, rotating her hips to tease both of them with pleasure, spreading her thighs to take him even deeper.

His hand slid from stomach to mound, his fingers gathering her wet heat before playing with the button of nerves that pulsed at her apex.

"My cock, deep inside you, fucking you until you come, then fucking you more. I can't get enough of you."

Shifting positions in continual harmony, they pleasured each other into oblivion, afterward lying entwined in a sweaty heap.

"Good night, Ellie." Cyrus brushed his lips over the nape of her neck. His snores lulled Eleanor to sleep.

When she woke the next morning she was alone in the bed. It was still early, the eerie feel of half dawn hung over the ranch. She had no idea where Cyrus was or what had jarred her awake. She had the coffee on and perking when he came through the back door, a smug expression on his face.

"I've been busy while you lollygagged in the bed." Cyrus crossed to the sink where he scrubbed and bragged.

Eleanor set a mug and a plate of toast on the counter and looked admiringly at him, waiting for him to elaborate.

"Had to help Bonfire. She dropped her foal in the middle of the night." He grinned proudly as if he'd fathered the newborn horse.

"Was it a difficult birth?" Eleanor had often wondered about the birth process. Like so many other areas of female information, it remained a mystery to her. Since Cyrus had no reluctance in discussing anything, she asked.

"Nope, mare and filly are doing fine." He slid his arm around her shoulders, giving her a quick squeeze. "Come to the barn and see my progeny."

"I have breakfast to fix."

Ignoring her halfhearted protest, Cyrus ushered her to the door. His arm remained snugly around her, matching his steps to hers so they walked in tandem. He smiled down at her, guiding her into the barn where he presented mother and daughter as if they were royalty.

Eleanor leaned over the stall gate and watched the filly suckle, feeling stirrings of hunger in her womb.

"Pretty picture, isn't it?" Cyrus' thigh was molded to her hip and he hugged her close. "Come back to bed," he whispered the words in her ear.

"Breakfast…"

"God, I like the feel of you in my hand." Without the constricting corset it was easy for him to thumb her nipple through the material, teasing her to give in.

"Please me," he coaxed, nibbling on her neck, sliding his hand up to cup her breast.

"Mr. Burke, it's daylight." Her protest was halfhearted at best.

"Not quite yet." He hustled her back inside the house and up the stairs before she could resist further. "Hurry and we'll catch the last of dark."

Eleanor slid out of her dress, ready to feel his weight and heat again. He always made her want. Cyrus stripped quickly and joined her on the mattress, parting her legs and entering her with a growl of pleasure.

Play with me… Eleanor twisted under him, glorying in the sensations. His chest brushed her nipples sending a flash of desire pulsing to her core. The walls of her channel gripped him, flexing and squeezing around his shaft.

She loved his intense expression as he thrust in and out of her, taking his time. Eleanor claimed his lips, touching her tongue to his when he opened for her.

She felt a giggle escape when he rolled them over, seating her astride. His shoulder muscles bunched under her hands and his shaft thickened when the tips of her nipples caressed his chest.

Give this up? Her heart clenched at the idea.

He took her nipple between his lips, biting the end enough to get her attention. "Harder?" Teeth and lips tugged on one peak while he pulled and twisted the other with teasing fingers.

Her cunny flexed and her hips rocked, carrying him deeper. She cradled his head as he suckled first one breast and then the other. Settling her thighs wider, she ground her soft flesh against his groin and he growled his approval.

He rolled with her to the side of the mattress, stood, and positioned her legs over his shoulders before entering her again. His hips jerked a staccato rhythm that drove his groin against her pearl until she shattered, her release triggering his. The hot pulse of his spill flowed into her body and she arched upward, her womb greedily capturing his seed before he lowered her legs and collapsed on top of her.

Hugging him in her arms, she whimpered moans of satisfaction against his chest.

When he levered himself high enough for her to see him, he looked as groggy as she felt. He stared at her as though seeing her for the first time. Self-consciously, she brushed her damp hair from her forehead.

"Goddamn, Ellie, that was good. I didn't slap on a condom before we... We need to talk—"

"No we don't. Your lapse is of no concern, Mr. Burke. I've been found barren by the best physicians in Hartford." Eleanor cut off his words, more shaken than she cared to admit when she escaped to the bathing room.

As she checked her appearance in the beveled mirror, her bottom lip quivered. She had to remind herself he was a scoundrel who was negotiating for cheap domestic help, not a man in love. For a moment she'd let herself slide into decadent forgetfulness.

Cyrus lay on the bed breathing hard, trying to figure out what had just happened. She'd turned to ice when he'd confessed his slip. Slip, hell—nothing had ever felt so right as when he nudged into her bare and naked the first time during the night. The second time had been premeditated bliss. Ellie brushed his attempted promise aside as if it mattered not at all.

He heard her go downstairs but lingered above, taking extra care shaving and getting ready for town. He missed her caustic remarks. *Now that I think about it, she's been quiet for a couple of days. Not mad, just not her usual mouthy self.*

In the kitchen, he poured himself a cup of coffee and continued the conversation she'd brushed aside in the bedroom. "I doubt the doctors in the East are any more competent then the bankers and other nabobs. I'd take their findings with a load of salt, Ellie."

"Then you better wear a condom when we have relations," she said flatly, ignoring him when he got in her way.

"Might be too late for that," he drawled, surprised at how much he wouldn't mind if it were so. "It only takes once, you know. You don't want a baby?" The thought made him frown inside.

"A child would be nice," she said, elbowing him out of the way so she could ice down one of the boxes he'd just put in the wagon. It wasn't exactly the response he'd been expecting.

"Well, I just want you to know if my seed takes root, I'll let you throw your rope around my neck." As soon as he said it, he recognized it as the lame-brained proposal it was. So did she.

"Very eloquently tendered, Mr. Burke, but your concern is unnecessary. Now would you bring that last box out here?" She glanced up, giving him her best *you're a jackass* look.

She dodged the conversation and kept him loading her pastries until the last carton was in the wagon. Then she stood waiting for him to leave. He wasn't ready yet. She looked at him, he looked at her and finally he asked, "You upset about something?"

"Not at all," she said, folding her hands in front of her.

He caught a blonde strand of hair escaping her sedate bun. Rolling it between his fingers, he bent close, inhaling the scent of lilacs and blanketing his senses with Eleanor before he left for town.

He nipped her neck, then kissed it. "Our two-week trial period is over today." It seemed as if she'd always been a part of his life. Suddenly anxious to secure her stay, he asked, "You good with extending the contract?"

Cyrus hadn't doubted what her answer would be — until she hesitated.

"If you're offering me continued employment for four more weeks — yes. Then our business arrangement will end." Noticeably disinterested in the topic, she pushed the conversation back to her damn pastries. "It's going to be very hot soon. Could you..."

Irritated at the way she kept dodging his subject of choice, Cyrus climbed on the wagon. Hell, he wanted her forever but was begging for four more weeks.

"Don't forget to have Mable fill this order or I might have to serve beans for a week." Eleanor stepped closer, tucking two slips of paper into his shirt pocket.

"I'll be back in time for supper. What do you want me to bring you?" he asked gruffly.

"Just deliver my note to Mable. Everything you need is on it. And don't forget the spools of thread, the buttons and the new broom I listed."

"What happened to the broom you had? Maybe I can fix it," Cyrus offered.

"You can't. Pinch pennies on luxuries not necessities," she said piously.

"Guess I better get a new broom then." He was pretty sure he could fix it and not waste money but her disgust was apparent so he humored her, trying to get her to smile.

"What's the thread for?" he asked.

"Your shirts have so many buttons missing I've used all my sewing supplies. Whoever kept house for you before did a deplorable job. You need to pay more attention to your female employees' *domestic skills* in the future, Mr. Burke." Her smile was so bright her eyes seemed to glitter.

He drawled, "I'll do that, Eleanor."

He didn't pick up the reins to leave the ranch yard until he saw her go in the house. Then he started for town, replaying their negotiations in his head. *Our business arrangement…*

153

It jerked him to a skidding halt. *Armor, that's what's different — before she was open and having fun. Damned if she doesn't have her corset strings pulled tight again.*

Cyrus was still mulling over Eleanor's aloof expression when he neared the town's only store. He had some questions for Mable and he expected answers.

He unloaded Eleanor's desserts and carried them to the back, setting them near the coffee brewing on the small cookstove. The clerk gawked at him as usual and as always he winked, sending her scurrying as though the devil offered her temptation.

Mable was busy with customers and Cyrus helped himself to the dry goods and essentials on the list Eleanor had sent, boxing them and tallying each item for the final bill. Finished with his have-to-haves, he poured himself a cup of day-old brew and carried the mug with him as he studied the women's items for sale.

"Put this on my bill with the rest of the order," he told Mable when she joined him. He handed her his total, Eleanor's note and a heavy wooden rolling pin. Lowering his voice, he got down to real business. "Why'd you bring her to the ranch?"

"Because I know she can handle anything you throw at her and she needed a place to stay. Henry may work for you, but he takes orders from the family in Hartford and they sent for her. Right now, he thinks she's on her way home." Mable met his hard glance with her toothy grin, read Eleanor's note and said, "You want everything on this list?"

"Did I not say so?" Cyrus brushed aside her question, thinking instead about what he'd been *throwing* at Eleanor. She'd handled it all right, but he didn't figure Mable would appreciate how well.

"Give this to her. It's her cut from her last sales." Mable handed him a wad of greenbacks.

"You chargin' her full price for her ingredients?" Cyrus tucked the money in his pocket as he asked.

"You managing her business interests now?" They faced each other in a standoff until Mable conceded. "Wouldn't do her or me any good to build a business she can't make money at—of course I'm discounting for her."

"She wants that shack next door fixed up. Don't suppose it was your idea was it?" Cyrus knew damned well who put Ellie on to the building.

"Didn't see you doin' it for an old lady like me, but I thought maybe those purple eyes of hers might melt a layer from your gold-encased heart."

"Put the lumber on my bill and get some locals workin' on it. She wants to open for business in a month." He'd already decided Eleanor was staying on the ranch. He'd promised her the shack would be ready for business. He just hadn't promised she'd be running it. All in all, he'd decided another round of negotiations was imminent.

"Preacher still needs a new roof on the church. While you're feeling so generous, you might want to donate to the cause." Mable followed him to the wagon, nagging him about another one of her pet projects. She'd been after him to help the church get a new roof for over a year. They could drown when it rained for all he cared. The churchers had slammed the doors on his mother when she'd birthed him—a bastard.

"Tell the preacher to come sling hash in my kitchen and scrub the floors for six weeks. If he works as hard as my current housekeeper, then we'll see. I've got no more time or money to waste on roofing the church now than I did the last conversation we had."

"Let Eleanor know I'll need the order doubled again come next Wednesday. I swear I can't keep her bake goods long enough to take a bite out of one myself." Mable knew when to cut her losses and changed the topic back to Eleanor.

"Mable, do you have any idea how many cream puffs she's going to have to sell to make a living? Hell, she'll work dawn to after midnight and wear herself out. What are you thinking putting this idea in her head?" Cyrus might keep his opinion under wraps with Eleanor but he sure as hell didn't hold back with the store owner.

"She's got nothing waiting for her but trouble at home. What other option does she have?" She looked at him shrewdly and waited.

"Eleanor has other choices." He slapped the reins and set the rig in motion.

"That old building next door needs a lot of work. I'm not cuttin' the cost of nails for you. Understand that," Mable called after him.

Cyrus drove away thinking about the shack Eleanor intended to call home. It wouldn't be needed. He frowned. His plan to extend her stay to forever was meeting resistance.

"She's got her hat slapped on straight and she's packing her recipes. Guess I'll have to change her mind." He was relishing the coming siege as he drove the wagon into the ranch yard midmorning.

When he entered the house, he checked out her mood. Yep, Ellie was hiding and Mrs. Prim 'n' Proper had replaced her in the kitchen.

"I looked over that building you're whining about. Lumber to fix that old shack won't come cheap." Cyrus decided to dangle some bait.

It tickled Cyrus when her polite indifference immediately changed to militant attention. Miz Prim disappeared and Ellie prepared to wrestle as many concessions from him as she could.

"I would like to negotiate a continuing lease on my building." Her chin went up a notch.

"It's not your building and it needs new siding and a roof. You'd better think about that cost first." He scratched his jaw and frowned.

"Perhaps you can factor the cost of repairs into the rental you charge," she suggested.

"So you do know it belongs to me? And you played me a little, getting me to the fix-it-up stage?"

"Perhaps I *scoped out the lay of the land* before beginning my negotiations." She conceded, her lips curving into a satisfied smile.

Cyrus had an uneasy feeling he'd used just those words recently.

Chapter Eight

Eleanor enjoyed serving Cyrus his own words. She went to the porch to begin carrying in the supplies and he followed. He handed her a broom and stacked his own arms full of dry goods. As soon as they were through the door, she set down the broom and grabbed the top sack of flour, her grunt of surprise escaping as the weight pulled her arms downward.

"Mr. Burke," she panted, gripping the flour sack inches above the floor. "Your load is too heavy. You take on too much."

She half carried, half dragged the bag into the pantry, emptying its contents into the metal flour bin. White powder floated in the air around them as Cyrus set two more bags by her feet with a thump.

"Mable said to give you this." He pulled a roll of bills from his pocket and handed them to her.

Eleanor counted the bills, excitement tingling through her, barely paying attention to him.

"Quit your money-grubbing for a moment and listen to me."

"No." She looked up from her counting long enough to duck under his arm and scurry toward the exit.

Cyrus followed her, determined to have his say. "We've got some things to discuss."

"No we don't," she said quickly. Eleanor stood in the middle of the kitchen clutching her money in her hand and facing him. She tried not to stare but when he leaned against the sink and crossed one ankle over the other, his denims drew tight, clearly outlining the ridge of his arousal. She ignored the hungry clench of her womb and pointed outside.

"I have supply boxes to empty and supper to fix. You're taking up needed space in my kitchen." Then she remembered it wasn't her kitchen and flushed. "I beg your pardon—your kitchen—but I can't work with you in the way."

She had to be firm. Cyrus was heady—like fine wine. Rough cowboy on the outside he might be, but he knew how to please a woman and under his gruff exterior lurked the skills of a consummate lover. She wanted to succumb—take whatever he offered and savor it as it developed.

It was hard to remain aloof but Eleanor reached in her pocket for strength, fingering the purple garter, a gaudy rose-topped reminder that she was one of many housekeepers who'd tended his needs and served him night dessert. That he was willing to marry her to get the addition of a clean house — well, that was an insult.

"I found a present for you at Mable's store."

Eleanor waited expectantly, preparing for some licentious memento he might offer — a silk scarf, sensuous robe, fancy garter?

"Thought I'd get you something you can use in your pastry business." Cyrus turned, rummaging in one of the boxes on the counter before handing her a wooden rolling pin.

"Thank you." Eleanor accepted the work tool, blinking in astonishment at the gift, her disappointment warring with relief that it hadn't been the usual fare. Actually, it was a thoughtful present. Mable's old hand-me-down had one grip gone and it made rolling thin piecrust a lot more work.

"About the other," he said. "The rubber…"

"Use them as you would with all your other housekeepers. I would not want you to worry nor me to be compromised." His segue from pastry tools to his condom lapse startled her so much she didn't guard her speech.

He started to say something then pulled his hat on instead and Eleanor found herself squeezed in a tight embrace, her body molded to his as he kissed her.

"I don't want to use them again," he growled, nipping up her neck and rubbing his jaw against her cheek. "From now on, I want to feel your wet heat squeezing my cock up close and personal."

She was in complete mental disarray when he left. To compose herself, she counted her pastry money and made notations in the account ledger he'd provided. *Is he trying to get me with child to secure his housekeeper?* The thought was too silly to entertain for long.

Eleanor set aside her pastry business to take care of her housekeeping duties, shelving the supplies, peeling the potatoes for supper and making three dishes of peach cobbler for dessert. As she rolled out the thin crust she smiled in appreciation at the thoughtful gift Cyrus had given her.

Then she remembered the scarves upstairs in his chest and grimaced. Looking for something else to focus on, she put the cobblers in to bake and sat in the porch swing sketching the interior shelving she'd need in her shop.

Her thoughts were interrupted when Aunt Millie and Uncle Henry, accompanied by Mable sitting in the back seat, arrived in their buggy. Fine conveyance though it was, the rough trip from town to the Burke land had coated it and its passengers in dust.

"An Alcott selling her services as a domestic. Eleanor, what can you be thinking? As soon as I returned to town and saw your pastries in Mable's store, I knew you hadn't left, and everyone else will too." Millie immediately began her harangue when the carriage stopped.

With the assurance of a job backing her, Eleanor said tartly, "It became apparent I needed to find a means to support myself when Uncle Henry confiscated my funds—I have done so."

Uncle Henry said, "Eleanor, calm down. I admit we were a little precipitous in ordering you back to Hartford. My apologies, my dear, but Millie's right. It won't do at all, you working as a housekeeper for Burke."

Damnation. She cursed silently. She'd secured her grubstake with continuing employment from Mr. Burke—now was not the time for her relatives to descend and try to wrest control from her.

"Excuse me," she said. Grabbing the mallet, she beat the gong resoundingly, signaling trouble. With the sound still reverberating in the air, Eleanor announced, "I have cobbler baking," and retreated to the kitchen to retrieve her dessert from the oven. When she returned, the three uninvited visitors were still in the buggy and Cyrus was riding into the ranch yard.

* * * * *

"You've got company on the way to the house." Sage had found Cyrus in the back pasture stringing wire and delivered the bad news. "Looks like the bank president and his wife with Mable Smyth riding in the jump seat."

Unease simmered in his gut. Mable knew better than bringing unwanted visitors on his land. Something was wrong.

"Can't have trespassers harassing my cook. Take over here." He'd left Sage in charge and headed for home. The length of Eleanor's employment was something he'd been trying to discuss with her—as in she wasn't leaving. The possibility of losing her today worried him all the way to the ranch. As he neared the barn lot, he heard the trouble gong booming. *Sounds like she's callin' for backup.*

His thoughts were grim but he made his tone amiable when he approached the group frozen in discord. Eleanor stood on the porch facing the Alcotts and Cyrus stopped his horse on their other side so they had to divide their attentions.

"Middle of a workday is a strange time to come for a visit, Henry. Is there a problem at the bank?" Cyrus folded his arms over his pommel, leaning forward sociably. Henry wasn't fooled at the show of congeniality and flushed red.

164

"Eleanor, you will ruin us all. If not your own reputation, please have a care for ours." Henry's wife ignored everyone but Eleanor.

"Gossip's an ugly critter, Millie. I'd be careful. It has a way of doubling back with a bite sometimes." Cyrus pinned Millie with a warning stare before pulling out his pocket watch to study it.

"As you know, Henry, finding good help isn't easy. It would be a shame if I had to waste valuable time finding a new bank president."

"Let me explain," Henry began his stumbling justification. "My wife and I just learned...we've come to fetch our niece...there's been a misunderstanding. She can't be your housekeeper." His last sentence was delivered frantically.

"It won't do, not at all." He shook his head, looking desperate.

"Mrs. Lacey and I have a contract. You figure on buying it out?" Cyrus drawled.

"Yes," Millie snapped.

"Mrs. Lacey, are you good with that?" Cyrus shifted his glance to Ellie, who looked ready to take off running.

He'd seen Eleanor's anger, humor and disdain, but until now, he'd never seen her fear. She stood blanched of color, hands fisted at her sides, facing all of them defiantly. It disappointed him some that she had no faith in him.

"I am *not* good with that, Mr. Burke. I have a contract with you and our agreement states that you will deal only with me. I believe I have several more weeks of employment to complete." Her head tilted proudly as she answered him.

"So you do." He nodded agreement.

Eleanor got some color back in her face, apparently made confident by his oblique support. Cyrus hid his smile when Eleanor faced down Henry.

"Uncle Henry, Mr. Burke and I have made an agreement concerning the building next to the Smyth Mercantile. When funds are needed for repairs and supplies, please transfer money from my allowance to my employer's account."

Cyrus was proud of her. Emboldened by witnesses, Eleanor did well, maneuvering Henry into looking like a thief if he said no.

"Guess that ends the conversation, Henry. Have a safe trip back to town." Shrugging and displaying indifference he didn't feel, Cyrus cut short any protest the banker might make.

Henry's wife wasn't so obliging. She scrambled from the buggy and was already on the steps to the house before either man could stop her.

"Where the hell do you think you're going, Millie?" Cyrus asked gruffly.

"I'm afraid I need to use your convenience, Cyrus." She turned her head, smiling triumphantly at him from the porch.

"Is that apple or peach cobbler Eleanor's fixing?" Mable asked, sniffing the air.

Cyrus didn't miss Henry's wistful glance at the front door.

"Melts in your mouth," Cyrus taunted him. "My housekeeper's a hell of a cook." He wet his lower lip as if tasting the memory and asked, "You ever had one of those things she calls éclairs, Henry?"

"Eleanor has a fine hand with pastries. We agree on that. But we both know a woman of her station shouldn't be living here and working as your housekeeper." Alcott punctuated his statement with a stiff nod.

"I'll cut you some slack this time, Mable, because you put Mrs. Lacey up when this jackass booted her out. Next time though, you bring unannounced visitors to my ranch and you lose the padlock key."

"Cyrus, that's a load of hoo-ha Henry's feeding Eleanor. He's got another ticket for Hartford in his vest and those are her trunks we brought along. He's taking her to the train depot in Paris. Not back to town." She pointed at the baggage tied to the back of the buggy and tattled.

"That right, Henry?" Cyrus looked at the banker, who met his gaze defiantly.

"Eleanor was sent to our home for safekeeping. Her presence is now required in Hartford. I haven't been given the details, but the divorce is now a dead issue, buried with William Lacey in his grave. I understand my niece's reluctance to return, but she can't hide forever and I must oblige the head of the Alcott family when he issues his orders."

His expression—militant and set—reminded Cyrus of Eleanor when she'd refused to give up Mable's business.

"I guess you Alcotts are a big deal in Hartford?" Mable inserted herself in the standoff.

Cyrus had done his homework and knew they were.

"The Alcotts are a family of importance and responsibilities. Scandal undermines business. An attack on one member is an offense against all." Henry elevated his chin proudly. "We are seeking redress for Eleanor's insult."

"Those are mighty fine words, Henry. You forget that when I hired you we agreed that my business came first?" Cyrus drawled the words slowly, watching red creep up the other man's neck and reach his chin.

"I am a loyal and trustworthy employee and I work very hard managing your business affairs as well as the bank's. I believe you have found my investment advice valuable and we have found consensus on most issues. But on this we must disagree. Eleanor has been ordered home."

"Whatever your family is paying you, double it and add it on to your current salary each month." Cyrus figured money talked first with Henry.

"It's a most generous offer, one that I would be happy to earn, but I must decline if the offer includes my niece's continued habitation with you on your ranch." Henry looked so depressed Cyrus almost felt sorry for him.

"I proposed," Cyrus told him flatly. "She's considering it. Don't get in the way."

"You proposed marriage?" Henry asked in disbelief.

"Yep." Cyrus caught the flash of Mable's grin as she nodded her approval. He switched his attention to the store owner and asked, "How's her business doin'?"

"She'll have folks waiting on the day she opens up and that can't be soon enough. The dessert customers are beginning to take up room in my store and crowd out my shoppers."

"I thought you said you were getting married," Henry said suspiciously.

"I said I offered."

"Then why set up the building for her?"

"A person likes to have choices. I figure if I can't come in first with Eleanor in a runoff between me and a goddamned cream puff filled with air, I don't deserve to have her. Like I said, she's considering me. Meanwhile, she's my housekeeper as long as she wants the job."

"Henry, nobody knows she's here. If anyone asks, tell 'em she's been called back to Hartford to take care of her late husband's estate," Mable suggested.

Cyrus noticed the way Mable packaged the lie inside the truth.

"And my father—Eleanor's grandfather—what do you propose I tell him?" Henry eyed both of them grimly.

"Tell him to go to hell and back," Cyrus snarled. "He didn't take care of Ellie when he should have, and he's not getting the chance to mess her life up again."

Eleanor waited impatiently for Aunt Mildred to come downstairs. If she guessed correctly, her aunt lurked above, inspecting all the rooms while she had the opportunity. During the time Eleanor had been a guest in Millie's home, she'd complained more than once that she'd never seen the inside of Mr. Burke's house. It seemed certain she wouldn't miss this chance.

"I'm in the kitchen," Eleanor called when steps coming downstairs alerted her of Millie's return.

"I've put the coffee on in case Mable and Uncle Henry come in for dessert." Aunt Mildred came into the room, looking around with interest. Eleanor cut one of the peach cobblers, already thinking about what to replace it with at supper time.

"You're really doing all of this work, aren't you?" Her aunt's tone was amazed as she caught hold of Eleanor's hand and turned it over, peeling back the work glove and displaying the new calluses on her palm.

"Of course. I told you, I'm earning the money to set up my pastry shop." Eleanor spoke matter-of-factly.

"You know, Eleanor," Millie said, a speculative gleam in her eyes. "Cyrus Burke is one of the richest men in the state. If you play your cards right, you could catch a fine husband."

"So now it's all right if I stay?" The hint of sarcasm was lost on Millie.

"Of course it's all right. If anyone questions your stay here, should they come to know of it that is, I'll attest to seeing your clothes in separate quarters. And I'll tell Henry to forget this nonsense of your returning to Hartford. Child, he needs to understand we have bigger fish to fry right here." She bustled around the kitchen chirping happily.

Aunt Mildred was energized in a manner Eleanor hadn't seen before. It was interesting that this branch of the family also flinched under Grandfather Alcott's whip.

171

"You have no idea what this could mean for Henry and me. *Your* family has treated our marriage with contempt. *I* am not considered worthy of an Alcott. Henry's father, your grandfather, refuses to let us move to Hartford — not that I would choose to do so — but the insult is reprehensible. With you married to Cyrus Burke, Texas social and business doors will open, Henry's banking career will advance and we will be out from under the family's thumb."

"I'll bring the cobbler to the dining hall." Millie held the pie dish aloft, making it clear she didn't plan on leaving without first having dessert. "Henry has been lamenting the loss of your baked goods ever since you left." Still carrying the dessert, Millie went to the porch and invited Henry and Mable inside.

Eleanor half expected a pointed suggestion from Cyrus encouraging Millie's departure, but he dismounted as Henry jumped down, helping Mable from the buggy before all of them came into the house.

Deferring to Cyrus as the host of the occasion, Eleanor waited for his direction. He surprised her again.

"Eleanor, would you bring the coffee in here and join us?" Instead of his usual familiar attitude, his demeanor was formal — respectful.

Coolly she retreated to the kitchen. Once behind the closed door, she gasped for breath. They were

172

all there, representatives of her past, future and now. She had an overwhelming desire to burst into tears and flee. She just wanted to be left alone.

Calming herself with one last gulp of air, Eleanor carried the coffee to the dining hall. As any good domestic would, she circled the table serving the guests before filling her employer's cup. He'd kept the chair next to him empty and waved her to the seat.

"I have cobbler to serve," she murmured.

Mable dished up her own before scooting the cobbler toward Millie who served Uncle Henry and then lifted a wedge to her own plate.

"Problem solved. Join us, please." Cyrus was polite but insistent.

Eleanor sighed and sat down.

In this setting, she saw the man others envied and feared. Gone was his playful manner, replaced by the stern man she'd met on her first day here. Uneasily she looked around the table and felt control slipping away from her.

Aunt Millie, basking in her inclusion at Cyrus Burke's table, smiled graciously, eating her dessert with dainty bites. Uncle Henry savored his cobbler but when her gaze met his, he looked toward Cyrus then back at her and frowned.

"Eleanor, you must return to Hartford." Refusing to cede control to Mr. Burke, Henry interrupted the quiet, pushing aside the false social atmosphere. As her only male relative present, her uncle delivered the family patriarch's edict.

"You'll have to convey my apologies to Grandfather. I won't be returning to Hartford, Uncle Henry." She shuddered under a wave of revulsion, tensely gripping the china cup until Cyrus pried her fingers loose. Then he poured her coffee, adding a dollop of cream the way she liked it. The intimate gesture wasn't lost on her or the others in the room as he radiated possessive authority.

Henry cut a bite of cobbler and studied it, his approving gaze sliding from the dessert on his fork to her before he continued. "On the other hand, Mr. Burke has explained that he has made you an offer of marriage."

It wasn't a question, but nevertheless he waited for her to confirm his statement.

"Are you marrying Cyrus Burke?" Aunt Millie burst out, not bothering to hide her excitement.

Out of sight of the others, Cyrus nudged Eleanor's foot with his, stretching beneath the table until his leg touched hers.

"Mr. Burke's offer is certainly flattering." Her tension disappeared and her voice was serene when she answered.

I'll let you throw your rope around my neck. She imagined throttling said neck and avoided looking at him, seeing instead Millie's hopeful gaze.

"We haven't finished negotiating." His growled words were heard by all. She refused to let him fluster her now that she felt in control again. It was possible his foot anchoring her under the table and promising her support had something to do with her inner calm.

"Before decisions are made, I have to fulfill my contract as your housekeeper, Mr. Burke." Her words were a prim reminder of their status.

"So you do," he agreed.

Eleanor looked down the table and as she caught Mable's glance she was reminded of her business partner's earlier advice. *Don't let Burke get between you and your pastry shop.*

"I also have desserts to bake for Mable, my pastry business to plan, and building preparations to oversee." Her firm commitment resounded up and down the table, bringing frowns from her relatives and a beaming smile from Mable.

"The building will be ready." Cyrus' bland promise left her wondering what chicanery he was up to.

"As per my specifications," Eleanor reminded him.

"Exactly to your specifications, Eleanor." The underlying hint of laughter in his voice made her risk a quick peek at him. His expression remained that of a landlord negotiating terms but he rubbed his knee against the thick folds of her skirt, spreading warmth through her limbs to her core.

At this most inappropriate time, heat pooled in her lower regions, sending shivers of desire coursing through her.

"I have supper to prepare. I'm afraid I will have to bid you all good day." Eleanor stood and walked toward the kitchen door, pausing to speak to her pastry partner. "Mable, I'll double the order for Wednesday."

Not waiting for a reply, she continued from the room on unsteady legs, the power of her arousal magnified by Cyrus' gruff tones as he ushered the uninvited guests outside.

Chapter Nine

"I'll take Eleanor's things to her." Cyrus walked to the back of the buggy after seeing Millie seated and Henry behind the reins. He wanted them gone.

"What the hell did she pack in here?" He grunted, hoisting the big steamer trunk to his shoulder, groaning under the weight as he carried it to the porch.

"Everything she could bring from home, I expect," Mable told him. "Eleanor said she's never going back. It might make more sense to carry these back to my place."

"No." The word leapt from his mouth in a guttural snarl. He didn't need to say more when Millie inserted her opinion.

"Mind your own business, Mable. Eleanor will need her possessions. You sent her looking for a job and she convinced Mr. Burke to hire her. He's got no complaints and as far as I know, neither does she. Stay out of it."

Cyrus returned to the buggy, letting Millie have her say. He didn't have to look at her face to know there was a determined gleam in her eye. Good. He slid the second trunk from Henry's fancy conveyance, letting it land on the ground with a thump.

"Hope she didn't have any breakables in there, Cyrus, because if she did, they're broke," Mable scolded him.

Cyrus sneaked a quick look at the house hoping Eleanor hadn't seen him maybe smash her valuables. Raising his voice in case she was listening, he changed the subject. "Like I said earlier, Mable, get some men started on fixing her pastry shop."

"Like I told you earlier," Mable bared her teeth, her words mimicking his. "I've got no room for a full-time operation so you know I found carpenters as soon as you left. Since that shack's currently held together with rusty nails in rotten wood, it'll cost you a pretty penny to get the work done in time for her to set up shop."

"Don't spare the cost. Eleanor and I will negotiate an agreement that covers it in her lease." After Ellie came to her senses, Cyrus had a dozen men who'd pony up good money to rent the place once it was ready. It was a solid investment.

"No more uninvited guests. Remember what I said," he reminded Mable. She nodded agreement and Henry took up the reins, ready to head for home.

"Henry, about these allegations made against your niece." As far as Cyrus could tell, Henry was the closest male relative Ellie had protecting her, and so far, he'd made a poor job of it. He walked to her uncle's side for a final talk and could feel the ice frosting up in Alcott's veins as Millie's look changed to one of horror.

Before the two of them could babble stupidity, he said, "Shuffle some of my money around. See what you can free up to invest."

"In what?" Alcott asked, looking relieved at the fast shift in topic.

"Those four sonovabitches that lied about Eleanor—wipe them out and bury them alive." Cyrus dropped his amiable guise and let his rage show as he delivered his order.

"Oh my," Millie whispered.

"My pleasure." Henry's grim look softened to a smile. By the time he turned the buggy toward town, his expression had changed to thoughtful anticipation.

Cyrus stood watching the three unwanted visitors until they disappeared from sight. His heart thumped so hard he thought it might leap from his chest. Damn the Alcotts or anyone else who tried taking Eleanor from him. His thoughts were savage when she joined him on the porch.

"Here's your things. Hope to hell you're stayin' awhile because I don't relish hauling them more than once." He pointed at her trunks before wrestling the smaller one from the ground to his knees, then his shoulder.

"For goodness' sake, let someone help you with that. It took two men to carry each when they were loaded on the carriage at home."

"Easterners—what do you expect?" Cyrus snorted, ignoring her advice. By the time he got to the top of the stairs, he knew he should have listened. His back and shoulder hurt like hell. Not wanting to appear like a weakling himself, he went back for another shot of torture.

The second time he staggered up the steps to the spare bedroom, he felt the muscles in his back spasm. Grunting, he set the cumbersome box on the floor. When he straightened, he couldn't disguise his wince of pain. Eleanor spotted it.

"You've hurt yourself. I told you the trunks were too heavy."

"If you've got nothing better to do than stand around and watch me work, go sew some more buttons on," Cyrus snarled, in no mood for her *I told you so*.

She nodded and left the room without a word— until she hit the stairs. Her "yes, master," floated up to where he stood.

"That is one mouthy woman," he muttered, wincing around a grin as he tried to get the kink out of his back. He bypassed the kitchen and went out the front door, not eager for Eleanor to see the results of his stupidity. By supper he was taut with pain, easing into his chair at the table, trying to appear natural.

"What's got you all stove up, boss?" Pete noticed and asked.

"He carried my steamer trunks upstairs without help. It was a splendid effort but he hurt his back." Eleanor set a basket of rolls on the table and retreated before he could comment, not returning to the dining hall until the rest of the men had gone for the night.

"Pete said it works on horses." She set a bottle of liniment on the table. "It should be fine for a stubborn mule."

"That stuff burns like fire and stinks to high heaven. I don't need it. I'll be good as new by tomorrow." He glared at the bottle.

She nodded with no more argument, cleared the table so he could work and went to the kitchen. He enjoyed the sound of her puttering around but his back hurt too damned bad to go out and see what she was doing.

When he heard her slip up the stairs he was disappointed she'd not said good night. Then, as though remembering the oversight, in a few moments she descended partway and called to him.

"Good night, Mr. Burke. I hope your injury is better by tomorrow. I'll sleep in the spare bedroom so I don't disturb you. I appreciate your effort to deliver my trunks."

Cyrus glanced up to growl a good night and almost swallowed his tongue. She wore a filmy negligee, lavender in color, clinging in style. Plump swells of her pink breasts spilled over the beribboned bodice.

"Thank you for the rolling pin. I will always remember you when I roll out dough." She was a picture of demure innocence flashing him a smile that went straight to his groin.

I'll remember you when I roll out dough. What kind of memory is that? But then he had a mental image of Eleanor flattening pie crust with his kitchen tool in her hand and his other tool buried inside her. *Maybe just wearing an apron.* His cock saluted the idea.

Cyrus groaned loudly as if in dire pain.

In a flash, she came down the steps and stood beside him, smelling the strong contents of the bottle she held.

"Come here," he said, drawing her in front of him and removing the bottle from her hand. "I like this," he growled, smoothing the filmy folds of her nightgown over her hips.

"Let me make you more comfortable." She sank to her knees before him, stroking the rigid member tenting his pants before fumbling his belt open, freeing his cock so it stood tall and waiting. Ellie's mouth was wet and warm, better than any liniment or medicine she could have concocted.

Leaning forward, she ran her hands up his sore back, kneading the kinks from his flesh as she sucked him. He closed his eyes, groaning in pleasure as her lips and tongue danced along his turgid length before taking him deep in her throat. He came with a shout as her hands worked magic on his back.

Cyrus slumped weakly in the chair, stroking her hair, enjoying the way her head rested on his thigh. He was almost asleep when she stood and patted his arm.

"I need to put some liniment on you and wrap you tight."

"Just tie strapping around me," he muttered, wincing as he looked over his shoulder. Damned if she wasn't standing there with her lips swollen and her cheeks flushed, holding the bottle, still determined to have her way. For once, he had sense enough to keep his lips buttoned, it being obvious Eleanor would win this round.

"There, that should do it." After rubbing in the ointment and hurrying to get the strapping cloth tied on him, she stepped back and wiped her hands on a towel. "Slide your arm around my waist and lean on me when you're climbing the stairs."

Cyrus wasn't so stiff he couldn't make it up the steps on his own but he took her offer anyway. Draping his big frame over her shoulders gave him a chance to appreciate her rosy flesh peeking at him from lavender silk. Once upstairs, when she would have gone to the other room, he turned her in the direction of his.

"Our bed," he told her. "The damn trunks can stay where they are, but you sleep with me."

* * * * *

"Neither one of us will get any sleep if this continues." Eleanor sat up, preparing to move to the other room when Cyrus shifted for the fourth time

"Lie back down and curl around my back. Your heat might make it feel better," he coaxed.

"Mr. Burke, I think being a warming pad is a highly irregular housekeeping task," Eleanor teased him but obligingly rolled to the center of the bed and pressed her chest to his back.

"Go to sleep, Ellie." He put his arm over hers, holding her in place and cradling her hand on his belly.

Curled protectively around him, she whispered softly against his back, "Thank you for your help today."

His answer was little more than a grunt.

"How old are you, Mr. Burke?"

"Thirty-five," he said grimly, "and right now I'm feeling every one of the years."

Eleanor rubbed his back with her cheek, turning her face to plant a kiss on his shoulder. "So you've been alone a long time."

"Not by a long shot." He snorted at the idea. "I've got men who've been here on the ranch damned near as long as me. Beckett and I go back to the schoolyard. We fought each other on a regular basis until it got boring. Then we teamed up and took on others."

"And your mother...?"

"Rounded up wild strays with me to help me get my start. We did it together. She took sick right after I sold our first herd. I started the house and Sage pitched in, but we couldn't finish it in time for her to move in."

"I just wondered," she whispered snuggling closer, trying to absorb old pain and new.

Her support against his back seemed to be the only thing needed to send Cyrus off into snores. One arm was pinned under her side, the other on his abdomen under his big paw.

Her breasts, molded as they were to his back, were caressed by every breath he took. She squirmed enough to get her arm free, pillowed her head and tried to relax. Finally Eleanor fell asleep, her nose pressed against Cyrus' back, matching her breaths to the rhythm of his.

* * * * *

She woke at first light, her mind a disturbing mix of confusion. An offer of marriage from a man of Cyrus' stature would withstand even Grandfather's scrutiny. It was the simplest means of escape from the scandal she'd fled.

She pulled on her silk robe, glad to have access to her fine clothes again. Fingering the purple garter she'd pocketed, she studied Cyrus where he slept and squashed thoughts of practicality. She'd married William because it was the sensible thing to do and William had wed her to solidify his bank shares.

The fact that Cyrus prized her for her domestic skills, though somehow less offensive, still galled her. Washing quickly, she hurried to start breakfast, smiling as she contemplated her employer's maneuvering.

Foiled. Her grandfather's machinations were derailed by an autocratic cowboy. Her sense of humor — only recently discovered — displayed itself in occasional giddy laughter as she fixed breakfast, stacking the trenchers high and setting them out.

She banged the breakfast bell and then filled the coffee mugs before setting the pot next to Cyrus' chair. She avoided the dining hall after that, well aware that regardless of the bath she'd taken she reeked of liniment and him. Remembering his injury, she poked her head around the edge of the door to see if all was well and blatantly listened to his story. "She fixed up a hot pad and doused it with Pete's horse medicine." Cyrus rolled his shoulders and twisted his neck. "It worked."

"Eleanor, you're wearing more liniment than I am." He must have been listening for the door hinges to squeak. He held the empty coffee kettle out to his side, expecting her to take it while he continued his story.

She refilled the pot and returned it to the table in time to hear his latest declaration.

"I've offered Eleanor a permanent place here, boys. She's considering it." Cyrus scooted the coffeepot down the line, avoiding her gaze.

"Good." Bill grunted his opinion, speared a pancake and lifted his cup, saluting her.

"Better mind your manners, boss. We've got a lot riding on this deal." Pete grinned, motioning at the food on the table.

Playful teasing and respectful glances were cast her way as she retreated to the kitchen and stayed there.

"You gonna hide in here all day?" Carrying a load of dirty plates with him, Cyrus joined her after the rest of the men left.

"Mr. Burke, what are you doing?"

"Helping you clear up," he answered, ignoring the real question.

"You're forcing the issue. You've told Uncle Henry, Aunt Mille—who you know can't help gossiping—and Mable about your ludicrous offer.

Now you've misled your ranch crew, suggesting that I may remain after payday. Why are you doing this?"

"I'm taking precautionary measures." His expression changed to serious.

"For what?"

"Just protecting your future," he said gruffly.

"My future is secure, thanks to this employment. It's unnecessary to publicly link our names. Actually, I would prefer that you don't. "

"Nope. I told Henry to go ahead and draw up the marriage contracts early just in case something happens to me. I don't want you left high and dry with a kid in your belly."

"Did you not hear me tell you I'm barren?" Eleanor stared at him, dumbstruck.

"Yep."

"Well?"

"We'll just keep my offer pending until we find out. If you're not carrying when you leave, you've got a pastry shop waiting. If you are, you'll be staying here and it's Mrs. Burke you'll be."

"What if I don't want to marry you? As a matter of fact, having considered it, I don't want to marry anyone." That wasn't really true. Under the right circumstances she felt that Cyrus would make an excellent husband.

"Is that right?" His lips twitched as if he held back laughter. "We can get married and pretend to live in sin if that helps you out any."

"Don't be an idiot."

"I'll leave no bastards behind when I die, Eleanor. My mama and pa jumped the gun and before he could make it right for her he got himself killed. That's not happening to you and me." His words were devoid of his usual humor as he spoke of his father, a man he'd never mentioned before.

"Who was your father?" she asked hesitantly.

"John Cyrus—whether he would have married Mama or not is a moot point, since he died in a flashflood before he knew I was to be."

"Did his people help her?" Eleanor shivered, considering the horror of a young girl discovering she was with child and alone.

"Hell, no. Painted her a trollop and turned their noses up. My grandfather Burke had a little spread east of here. That's where I grew up."

"And your father's people? Where do they live?"

"They moved on," Cyrus said nonchalantly, picking up one of the hot pecan sandies she'd just removed from the oven and blowing on his fingers. "I bought their land at auction. This part of my ranch is the first parcel I added."

"I thought you said you built this house," Eleanor said.

"I did. I took a sledge hammer to the old building, knocked it down and used some of the lumber from it to improve the barn. I built Mama a fine home in its place."

In spite of his mild words, Eleanor recognized the underlying ruthless revenge he'd exacted. Cyrus Burke was not a man to trifle with and she felt as though his story was a warning in itself.

"Though I better appreciate your concern for me, your gallantry isn't necessary." Eleanor assured him, side-stepping the real issue—her leaving.

"Anyway, have to or not, I think you should marry me and save me from the dire humiliation of being turned down." Cyrus scooped up three more sandies and as Eleanor watched, he bit into one of the confections, chewed the pecan sandy, swallowed and licked his lips. "Where the hell else am I going to get cookies like this straight from the oven?"

"My pastry shop." She beamed. "Mr. Burke, with all due respect, I found marriage stifling and have found not being married very liberating…"

It was difficult completing her point as he savored the cookie, listening to her attentively. She wanted to tell him that she refused to be married because she was a financial asset or a good cook. Instead she shrugged and said, "I've discovered that a widow has options."

"I kind of figured that out, Eleanor. But I've got some time yet to convince you that marriage to me would be your best choice and a whole new kind of liberating." Dusting off his hands, he closed the space between them and brushed his lips across hers before pulling on his hat as he walked to the door.

"I'm moving the herd to the east pasture today. I won't be in until supper. Don't work too hard. We've got some playing to do tonight."

"Your back?" she asked.

"Medicine last night did the trick," he said, winking at her before he left.

When she was alone, she pictured the young Cyrus Burke with a wrecking bar, demolishing his father's home. Underneath the playful exterior was a will of iron. She should just say yes to his offer and be done with it. She would have a beautiful home, a rich husband and a good life.

I had a beautiful home, a rich husband and a good life. She frowned and shook her head. In retrospect, she'd had nothing.

Cyrus was pleased with his plan. He had her uncle's blessing. Now he had to convince Eleanor to marry him and harbored little doubt he'd win in the end. *Hell, she can't be living in the back of a store. I'm doing her a favor.* On that thought, he frowned.

Eleanor didn't act as though she was flattered by his offer. Instead, she seemed irritated. Maybe she didn't see him as a catch because she was the

191

real deal—a lady of quality. On the other hand, she didn't blink twice at him being a bastard.

Early on it had been an issue. He'd found that money made most problems disappear. Since he'd grown rich, he'd been stalked by every respectable and not so respectable woman in the county and other parts of the state. It was disconcerting when his housekeeper didn't see him as a prize.

Somehow during the short time he'd spent with Eleanor, his lust had given way to satisfied contentment and tender concern. He didn't know why she didn't just grab up his offer. They were dynamite between the sheets, she liked his house and she needed someone to take care of her. He'd decided he was willing to take on the job—if that meant marrying her, so be it.

"She needs me," he muttered. Uneasily aware that he needed her too, he tried not to think about that half of the equation.

* * * * *

During the following weeks, his strategy became countering all of her talk about her dessert shop, independence and being a free woman with inquiries about how she would decorate his house.

"What kind of rug do you want for the front door?" he asked when she pored over her ledger, doing sums and figuring at the table after supper.

"Something pretty," she waved her hand at him, ignoring the bait.

"Brown. Mable's got a pile of mud-colored ones. That way the dirt won't show," he said judiciously, looking at her across the expanse. It was another irritant. Instead of sliding in next to him, she'd said she needed space to work and set up her evening business at the far end of the table.

Eleanor laid down her pencil, leaned back in her chair and folded her arms. "Buy two rugs, one for outside the door and another within as an attractive complement for the floor."

"What color?" She'd taken the bait. Now all he had to do was reel her in. Cyrus waited as Ellie studied the floor in front of the door.

"Purple," she said. "With pink roses on it."

He tried to picture it, not wanting to hurt her feelings since he'd asked her opinion. But— purple—with roses? He cleared his throat. "I don't favor purple much. Maybe—"

"My mistake," she interrupted him and shrugged. "I thought you did." Then she took up her pencil again, ending the discussion. "Make sure you have sturdy shelving built behind my counter."

Another night he brought up the curtains she'd mentioned and she waxed eloquent about green velvet hangings with silk scarf tiebacks. But after she finished describing her idea of fancy draperies, she brought the conversation back to her business.

It became a pattern. As the end of their six-week contract loomed near, Cyrus began to worry. He didn't want to go back to living in an empty shell—bad food, dirty dishes and unappealing women. Eleanor was perfect.

"Ellie," he murmured, brushing his lips across her damp skin when she lay in his arms one night. "You fit me like a glove—as if you were made for me." The problem wasn't convincing Eleanor to enjoy bed sports with him. It was making her understand they were special.

"Cats in the dark," she murmured, almost asleep, exhausted from their coupling.

He didn't know what she was muttering about in her dreams, but he was pretty sure she was wearing herself out. He considered hiring help for her, then knew he couldn't since it would get around damn quick she was his housekeeper.

He decided he'd let her rest at night, but he couldn't seem to get enough of her. No matter how much he promised himself each morning he'd abstain, selfish bastard that he was, he had to be inside her each night.

Worse, he was positive her pleasure wasn't pretend, but come morning, as soon as her feet hit the floor, she acted as if it had never been. She was helpful, industrious, serene, and somehow managed to make it clear each day—temporary.

"Sometimes the worst thing a person can get is what they think they want. Ellie might have to sleep in that two-by-four shack before she appreciates what I can give her." As he herded steers to the newly fenced pasture, Cyrus muttered ideas aloud, trying to figure the best approach to persuading her to accept his offer.

"She's got you talkin' to yourself now, boss. Better hurry up and get the halter on her before she gets away." Jake rode by teasing him.

"I'm working on it, Jake." Cyrus' thoughts were grim. Six weeks had sounded like a long time at its beginning but it was a week before payday and Ellie was still dodging his marriage proposal, focusing instead on her domestic duties and her pastry shop plans.

As the house came alive under her attentions, Cyrus praised the clean windows, her cooking, his ironed shirts and her growing bedroom skills, only to be answered each time with her distant smile and reply, "Thank you, Mr. Burke."

Her wardrobe, delivered the day of her emancipation from Henry's control, proved to be enthralling. The scent of expensive perfume mixed with Ellie wove a sensuous spell around him whenever he was near. It was no wonder he couldn't keep his hands off her.

Wednesday before payday, he rode into the ranch yard after work, determined to get the issue of her future resolved. At supper, she wore a dress he'd not seen before and it draped around into a little bustle in back. A fancy little apron accented her narrow waist and had the crew not been watching, he'd have run his hand under her skirts for a quick feel. As it was, he pictured her naked in the apron and wore a hard-on through the meal.

After she'd cleared the table for his bookwork, Cyrus studied his figures, waiting for her to emerge from the kitchen.

Eleanor took a seat at the far end, barely glancing at him, and he suddenly had had enough. His chair legs screeched his frustration as he stood and strode to her end.

"Eleanor, I think it's time you learned to say my name." Before she could sass, protest or lodge a complaint, he hauled her into his arms and started the climb to the bedroom.

"If you throw your back out again, Mr. Burke," she warned, "I'm not rubbing horse liniment on you. It smells."

"Nag, nag, nag," he grunted, tossing her up and catching her just to show her he could. "You've got the wife role down pat, now all you need to figure out is how to say your intended's name."

"Your name is Mr. Burke as far as I'm concerned," she corrected him, pushing at his shoulder. "You're my employer and future landlord. We have a short-term contract, after which I'm going into business for myself."

"You're going into the business of being Burke's wife if you've got my young'un in your belly," he informed her.

"You don't want a wife, you want an unpaid servant."

"I want *you*, Eleanor." He reached the top of the stairs and stopped long enough to silence her next argument with a kiss.

In the bedroom, Eleanor laughed at him when he used two of his neckties to tether her hands above her head to the headboard. If he'd used the scarves in the closet, she might have killed him. She tested the knot—it was loose enough for her to slip if she wanted. She remained captured, waiting for his next move. He didn't linger, shedding his shirt quickly. His denims, he left on.

"Say my name," Cyrus ordered her.

Eleanor scoffed at him. "Or what, you'll ravish me?" She stretched seductively, taunting him.

Cyrus leaned on the mattress with one knee. Her body rolled toward him as he slipped his hand under her dress, touching the silk stocking covering her limbs. With one hand, he removed her delicate kid shoes. The other hand caressed her ankle, his thumb rotating against the sensitive area.

Sliding his hands upward, he peeled her dress higher until it lay across her knees. The heat from his palms left a trail of fire making her womb clench. He paused as though feeling her inner walls tighten and squeeze. Lifting her hips, he roughly shoved her dress to her waist.

"Really, Mr. Burke, you have an unusual method of torture." Excitement flooded Eleanor, empowering her. He was wild for her tonight, rougher than usual and determined to have his name from her lips.

Holding her gaze, he caressed her rump before grasping her silk and lace pantalettes, skimming them down her legs to be discarded. Her stockings he removed slowly, his knuckles brushing a trail across her flesh.

"I like your fancy socks," he said, stripping them free. "They're real handy." He tied them around her ankles, adding a second layer of bondage as he bared her lower body for his gaze.

"Open your knees."

Eleanor parted her legs, letting them fall as wide as her bound ankles allowed. Her sex was revealed and he leaned closer, blowing a gust of warm air, making her shiver and clench. "Spread your legs wider for me," he directed.

Eleanor arched her back, planted her feet securely against the mattress, pressed her knees wider and jutted her hips high, watching as he lowered his head and parted her folds to taste her.

She moaned, incapable of hiding her pleasure. He held one hand under her rump, steadying her.

She thrust her hips upward watching him feast on her. But it wasn't enough. Her pearl pulsed, responding to every brush of his mouth.

Eleanor followed the torturous path of his lips, trying to entice him to the spot that shrieked in need. Instead, he nibbled and suckled his way to her entrance, licking the liquid heat trickling from her sheath.

He flicked his tongue in and out, bringing her to the brink of orgasm without completion. She writhed under him needing more. "Please," she groaned, begging him.

Abruptly he removed his support from her bottom, kissing his way up bare skin until he rubbed his face against her belly. Through a sensuous fog, Eleanor heard him growl, "Say my name."

Dazed, she stared up at him. Cyrus straddled her waist, holding her gaze as he reached behind to caress the curls on her mound, fondling her breasts with his other hand. Pressing the bodice lower, he exposed her nipples.

It was torture. She arched her back seeking relief as the tips of her breasts poked upward, ruby — the color of desire.

"You want my mouth again?" he asked her.

Eleanor moaned, "Yes, please."

Both hands came up to cup and stroke and squeeze. He suckled her nipples, biting and kissing, giving each his attention.

He moved higher until his chest pressed against her breasts and she rode his thigh positioned between her sprawled legs. As his tongue thrust in and out of her mouth, he kicked the silk ties from her ankles, settling himself deeper against her mound.

She writhed upward, trying to get free but her arms remained tied above her head. He rocked his hips against her lower body, sensuously teasing her. "Say my name."

"Devil," she gasped.

His laughter was a guttural sound in the room—both of them breathing heavily as if they waged a battle.

He rolled off her, lifted her legs over his shoulders, buried his face between her thighs and ate her, settling his lips over her pearl and suckling with strong pulls until she whimpered. Abandoning her at the crest of her release, he explored the sensitive flesh inside her cleft, tickling her with his tongue, teasing moans from her.

Finally he tongued her with deep thrusts until her orgasm swept over her in pulsating waves. Wiggling her hands free, Eleanor pressed her palms to his head, holding him in place as he suckled her honey and laved her folds leaving her limp and spent in his arms. The only sound in the room was the creak of the bed frame as he silently adjusted his position beside her.

As he rested his face against her belly, Eleanor lazily stroked his hair until he turned his cheek and blew a loud raspberry against her flesh. Tangling her fingers in his thick strands, she tugged, getting his attention. When he lifted his head, she caressed his jaw and spoke in a somber voice. "I will miss you terribly when I leave."

"Horse shit," he interrupted her, swinging his legs from the bed and standing. "You're not leaving and you damn well know it. Now say my name."

Eleanor shrugged off his command. "Mr. Burke, I'm your housekeeper, not your personal slave. Our intimacies have been invigorating and educational, but nevertheless, as you have made clear from the beginning, they were duties."

"What the hell are you talking about?" he growled.

"Am I correct when I say that you want a wife who will replace your need for a cook, maid, laundress and mistress?" She held up a finger for each, punctuating her remark.

"And what's wrong with that?" he asked her, his tone defensive.

"Nothing, Mr. Burke. It's a splendid offer. Were I desperate, I would certainly snap you right up. But," she paused, meeting his glance steadily before adding, "I'm not desperate."

"It's a damn good offer not many women would find fault with."

"I imagine a long and continuing line of applicants would agree. I'd rather have the security of four walls and a stove," she said, trying to keep the sarcasm from her voice.

"Four walls I own," he reminded her.

"There are other buildings," she warned back, determined not to let him intimidate her.

Chapter Ten

Eleanor moved into the guest room she'd never occupied and spent a fitful night pacing the floor. The next day he was polite, withdrawn and gruff, and his visits to the kitchen were infrequent. The silence grew between them until by Friday they weren't speaking at all.

After supper she finished the dishes while the ranch employees filed through the dining hall and received their pay. She listened to Cyrus find something nice to say to each man and exchange quips and jokes as he paid each wage in cash.

When the final man had departed and she was sure they were alone, she walked into the dining hall, symbolically took off her apron and stood before him.

His expression was amiable while he counted the bills slowly as though she doubted his honesty. When the last dollar hit her hand, he spoke. "Mrs. Lacey, you've exceeded all my expectations. You've set a new standard for my future housekeepers and their duties."

A cold chill slid down Eleanor's spine but she refused to be frightened by his implicit warning. *So he will replace me as soon as I go through the gate.*

"Mr. Burke, I appreciate the opportunity you have given me. Every aspect of our relationship as employer and employee has been a pleasure," she said quietly.

"Now that I'm not your boss any longer, you can call me Cyrus," he said.

She considered it aloud. "Mable addresses you in that manner, so do your friends, but as you are too near my age for such a familiarity between lessee and landlord, I think it would be best if I continue as we have."

"And would you like for me to call you Mrs. Lacey?" He tilted his head sideways, studying her.

"That would be best," she agreed.

"I've got books to finish up," he said abruptly. His voice was brusque, the usual glint of laughter in his eyes gone. "I hope your store satisfies you."

"Anything you build is unquestionably solid, Mr. Burke. I am sure the structure is everything I asked for," she assured him hastily.

"The building is exact to your specifications, right down to the sign," Cyrus growled. For a moment Eleanor thought she saw a hint of smug satisfaction in his eyes.

She said, "About the other concern—seed planting and such—it's no longer an issue." A blush climbed her cheeks as she told him.

He nodded acceptance of the news and she tried to see his true emotion but she couldn't decide whether it was disappointment or relief.

"I'll be leaving early in the morning with Mable after she drops off your supplies. I-I'll say my goodbye tonight." She ran out of words and reasons to prolong the conversation. "Good night...Mr. Burke."

He remained polite and aloof and bid her good night, calling her Mrs. Lacey.

After she climbed to her room, Eleanor lay awake, aware of the man who slept across the hall snoring loud enough for her to hear. She finally rose, dressed, tucked all of her possessions into her trunks and went to the porch swing to wait for Mable, who had agreed to come early.

Cyrus hauled the supplies inside the next morning as two of his crew carried Eleanor's trunks to the empty wagon. That done, he said his goodbyes.

"Mable, I'll be in to settle up soon. Mrs. Lacey, good luck with your business. Let me know if the building doesn't suit."

"Will you attend my grand opening?" Eleanor asked. He couldn't tell if that was something she wanted or dreaded. He remained uncommitted.

"If I can," he replied, walking away to the barn to saddle up so he didn't have to witness Eleanor leaving. He rode out to string fence before the wagon pulled out. He'd intended to ride along at least to the place where he'd first seen her, but found at the last moment he just couldn't.

Slim cooked his usual beans for supper, supplementing it with a loaf of the fresh bread Eleanor had left behind. The men ate in silence, nobody ready to mention the loss of their cook. Afterward he told Slim to go on to the bunkhouse. "I'll do the washup."

He didn't want anyone else messing up Ellie's kitchen and he made sure the floor was clean too. He didn't bother to climb to his bedroom, stretching out on the couch with a shot of whiskey and wondering if he'd handled things wrong.

Second-guessing wasn't something he indulged in, but, he'd been damned sure he could talk her into staying, and look where that had ended up. He'd built the shop to her specifications and even as slender as she was, she'd have a time fitting her personal gear as well as herself in the tiny space. He figured he'd look better to her every night she spent in the cramped quarters.

He didn't get much sleeping done, finally going out and watering the garden again, but the trip through the kitchen served only to remind him Eleanor was gone and wouldn't be baking any pecan sandies for him in the near future.

She had her grand opening on Tuesday and he missed it, though he let some of the boys off early so they could show their support. They came home telling stories of her success and sporting sacks of cookies. He was depressed.

He slept on the couch, dressing out of the basket of clothes Eleanor had left folded in the sitting room. He ate whatever Slim fixed and spent afterward doing cleanup duty in the kitchen. At night he stared at the figures in his account book wishing Ellie was sitting at the other end of the table.

He stayed away from town on Saturday, incapable of seeing Eleanor without kidnapping her and bringing her home. Come sundown, Jake came galloping into the ranch yard waving a note from Henry Alcott.

Cyrus read it. "Bank matters require your attention. Urgent." It was Saturday night. The bank was closed on Sunday. Alcott's message didn't say anything about Ellie. Whatever Henry needed would keep. He stuffed the paper in his pocket, poured himself a glass of whiskey and drank himself to sleep.

Sunday morning he finally forced himself up the steps to the bedroom they'd shared. When he opened the closet door, a figure loomed there waiting to scare the bejesus out of him. He reached for his sidearm but then his hand relaxed as he stared at the dummy hanging from a hook.

He scratched his head trying to remember when Eleanor had said, "I need a new broom. The old one gave out". The old broom now served as the body for her life-sized doll.

"Hell, that was at the beginning of the month." Cyrus studied the homespun mannequin with interest. "I remember her ordering those buttons. Wondered at the time why she wanted that color."

Lavender eyes looked at him beneath brows sewn in black thread. A thimble served as her nose. A castoff silk scarf was wrapped around the figure's neck and the green velvet robe he'd pitched in the back of his closet was now draped over fake shoulders loosely tied to display a pink corset beneath. Eleanor had devised two legs, stuffing white silk stockings with linens and decorating one with a purple garter adorned with a red rose.

"Well, damn," he muttered. Remembering her snide suggestions about purple rugs and green velvet drapes, gradually the tight constriction in his chest began to loosen and his frown changed to a full-blown grin. "Guess she was upset."

Mad at him or not, it put a whole new complexion on her departure. He looked at the dummy and read aloud the note pinned to the bosom.

"A uniform for your next housekeeper."

Eleanor's hat perched on the head, sitting at a jaunty angle. Along with the eyes and nose, she'd detailed the rest of the face. Rouged lips formed a bow around a piece of pink cloth forming a tongue that stuck out, mocking him.

"You have a sassy mouth, Miz Prim," Cyrus told the dummy.

It was Sunday and he had no excuse other than seeing Eleanor to make the trip to town. He moved the dummy away from his clothes and pulled out a suit he rarely wore, dressing with care before he set out to make amends. As he drove the ranch buggy to his gate, he met a ranch guard waving a note from Mable for him. He read it and slapped the buggy horse into a trot, cursing the jarring ride to town.

Once there, he pulled up in front of Eleanor's new store, jumped down and tied his team to the rail. The place was locked up tight with a sign announcing, "Closed for Sunday church." She'd pinned a menu to the front bulletin board advertising her éclairs and cookies. He went to the side entrance but knocking brought no response. In disgust, he listened to the church bells ringing down the street.

"Eleanor," he muttered, "I might have known you'd make a beeline for respectability. Right about now, you're probably passing out a list of your wares along with the church pamphlets."

Disgusted, he started to turn away when the door opened and Eleanor cast a quick look over his shoulder before ushering him in.

"Cyrus, how nice to see you," she said, closing the door and guiding him sedately toward the back of the store out of sight of the windows.

Miz Prim to the end. "The churchers are all singing hymns," he told her wryly. "Your secret's safe. Nobody saw me."

"Would you care for some coffee? Dessert?" She brushed dust from his shoulders and took his hat. "You look very nice, by the way. I've never seen you in a suit. What's the occasion?"

Well, there it was—time to do his belly-crawlin'. He followed her to her kitchen and sat at the little round table. Ellie being Ellie, she put the coffee on while he watched and rehearsed his words.

He didn't indulge in the cookies she set next to him, afraid he'd choke if he tried to swallow.

The brew finished perking and she filled two mugs. When she sat down across from him their knees touched. He shifted on his chair, trying to get his swollen cock situated.

"You didn't come to my grand opening," she said abruptly.

"Figured I'd just be in the way. The boys said you did fine." It was kind of dark in the kitchen with her curtains closed as they were, but if he wasn't mistaken he could see a shine of tears in her eyes.

"It was lovely. My éclairs have become my best seller, your pecan sandies are the next favorite. I had the shop decorated and—"

"Did you miss me, Ellie? I missed you." He didn't want to hear about her business success. He wanted to take her home.

"Yes," she said quickly. "If the offer is still on the table, I've decided to marry you."

"What happened to 'you're Mr. Burke, my landlord and I'm not desperate'?" His mouth got ahead of his brain and he spoke before he could stop himself. He hurried to add, "Not that I'm not pleased to hear you've come to your senses. What convinced you? The small quarters, right? I knew if I built them to your specifications they'd never suit you." Feeling smug he examined the narrow space between the shelving and the work counter in the kitchen.

"The shop is magnificent—perfect. But I-I don't want to sell the pastries. I just want to bake them."

"But you said you wanted to be a business woman. What about your shop?" Much as he wanted Ellie, he smelled a rat.

"I've decided to let Aunt Mildred run it."

He peered across the table at her suspiciously. "So you're already hiring help and you just opened your doors?" Fascinated, he watched her gnaw on her lower lip again before she answered.

"We've come to an agreement. I'll bake, Millie will sell, and Mable will carry a few desserts in her store to point the public at my shop. My aunt's excited."

"How are you going to bake the goods when you're married to me and living on the Burke ranch?" Cyrus crossed his arms, ready to maximize his demands since it looked as though their negotiations had resumed.

"You'll carry them every morning," she assured him. When his eyebrow went up, she changed it to, "Or someone can."

Before she could say anything else, a heavy pounding began on the front door.

"It's my grandfather's attorney." She looked nervous. "He's been prowling around this building all morning."

When Cyrus stood, ready to talk to the lawyer for her, she shook her head, herding him into her living quarters. It was dark in there too.

"Ellie," he asked, pulling her into his embrace. "You hiding in here?"

She leaned her head against his chest and circled his waist with her arms, not speaking. He didn't hustle her for an answer because he liked the way she felt hugging on him that way. He let her simmer, rubbing his chin against her hair while he stroked his hand up and down her spine. He couldn't help but notice she'd decorated real nice in here too.

A fancy chair and marble-top table sat in a corner of the room. A thick carpet covered the floor. Rich, plum-colored drapes decorated the tall window, the glass pane covered by sheers. Cyrus' glance stalled. He hadn't ordered that window.

"You come into some money?" He looked around puzzled. The room was as pretty as a picture. Two oil paintings hung on the wall above a small-sized couch.

"Of course not," she said. "My business is just getting off to a good start."

"Then how in hell did you afford this stuff?"

"I didn't. You did," she answered glibly. "Mable and I decided you were leasing a furnished building to me. That way I'd be able to concentrate my expenses on my ingredients.

"Is that right?" He didn't give a damn about the furnishings. But leverage was leverage. "Reckon you'll be baking cupcakes a long time to pay me back for your furnishings," he drawled.

"We'll negotiate," she answered, shivering when a shadow passed by the window.

Cyrus hugged her tighter. "Whatever fix you're in, I'll take care of it. What's the lawyer want?"

"Grandfather and his attorney arrived yesterday. Uncle Henry has allowed him to believe that I'm still at your house. Mable told him she'd contact you asking for permission to enter."

"I crossed paths with Mable's request on my way to town." Cyrus showed her the note. "Got one from Henry last night too. What's the fuss?"

"Millie says Grandfather's furious at my behavior. She scandalized him even more by selling my pastries yesterday while I remained unavailable. By now, I'm sure he suspects I'm here."

"Why didn't you ride out to the ranch yourself? It would have been faster."

"They were looking for me and..." Eleanor's lip trembled and her breath caught. "I-I was afraid you'd already found a replacement for me."

"Well, I didn't," he told her. "But marrying me to hide out from your family isn't a real solid reason for doing the deed, Ellie."

"It's more than that. I like the privacy of the Burke ranch. I miss your house, the work and, of course, the bedroom sports." Ellie ticked off her reasons and none of them made him happy.

"Is that it? You want to come home because you miss the house?"

"Well, why do you want to marry me?" Her expression was militant when she answered for him. "Hmmm, let me see—I believe you told Mr. Beckett I would be cheap labor. You want someone to cook, to clean, to warm your bed and rub your back at night."

Cyrus swallowed, wishing his tie wasn't tied so tight, almost like a noose around his neck. "I have feelings for you," he muttered.

"What kind of feelings?" she demanded. "Feelings that marrying me is a good business deal?"

He looked around the miniature suite and snorted.

She had the grace to blush. "I have feelings for you, also," she confessed to the floor. "I'm miserable without you."

"Well all righty then. I'm glad to know your life's a mess without me, because I sure as hell can't live without you." He swung her into his arms, bouncing her playfully. "This place got a bed?"

"Behind the screen." She laughed and pointed at the other corner.

Sure enough, a dainty little four-poster sat behind the fancy partition and Cyrus made short work of getting them out of their clothes and into it.

"Woman, I missed you," he said, savoring the slow slide of his cock through her heat.

Her groan of pleasure joined his as she ran her hands up and down his back the way he loved. Then she cupped his face and stared at him.

"Do you love me," she whispered. "Really love me? I don't want to be married in another business deal."

"I love you, Ellie." He held her gaze, his expression serious. "I can't ever replace you." He ducked his head, exploring her nipples with his tongue, sucking on one taut peak until her back arched and she bucked under him. "Do you love me?"

"Yes." When he brushed his thumb across her pearl her orgasm rippled over her and she curled in his arms, content as a kitten.

Cyrus breathed easy for the first time in a week. He pinched her rump to get her attention. "You're supposed to say it back."

"Say what?" she asked, yawning.

"Admit you love me," he ordered her. "I waited six weeks to hear you say my name, and that's still been damn sparing. Hell, I'm not waiting around for you to decide if it's decent to say 'I love you' back."

"Cyrus, I love you beyond reason when I should wash my hands of a cretin who keeps trinkets from former lovers on his closet floor." Eleanor pulled on his chest hair and glared at him.

Damn, he'd forgotten about that. "From the dummy you left for me, I thought that graveled you some." He grinned down at her. When she didn't smile back, he sobered up fast. "Ah, hell. I figured on finding use for the junk some time or another. Throw it all in the trash if you're done making dolls with it."

"There will be no more lovers." She sat up commanding him and though he'd just come, his cock twitched ready for more when her breasts bounced jauntily above him. "Just me, forever. Understand?"

"Understood," he agreed. "One opinionated, sassy female is enough for any man." He pulled her down, draping her over his body, enjoying the feel of her damp skin against his. "You coming home with me today?" His heart thumped anxiously waiting for her answer.

Before she could reply, a man's voice called from outside. "Mrs. Lacey, I know you're in there."

"Grandfather's man is back," she whispered.

"To hell with him. You marrying me today?" He ignored the noise, waiting for her to agree. He wasn't leaving her alone another day to think up more of his flaws.

"Yes, I'm coming home and this time I want a key to the gate," she said sharply. "When I left, I felt like I was being locked out of heaven."

"A key to the gate, the house, the safe, the bank account and to my heart. I'm all yours, sweetheart. Now let's go see what that damned fool wants and get this show on the road. You've got ranch hands waitin' for supper at home."

She wrinkled her nose at him and Cyrus was pleased to see the dimple reappear in her cheek as they fumbled into their clothes. When the pounding commenced again, he swept her alongside him toward the door, whipping it open and catching the beefy fist, stilling the noise.

"You're disturbing the peace," Cyrus told him, squeezing the other man's hand until he blanched.

"Mrs. Lacey, your grandfather needs to see you." The lawyer's expression was determined.

"Tell Mr. Alcott, *Mrs. Burke* doesn't need to see him, but will do him the courtesy of meeting with him at Mable's place in an hour." Cyrus ended the conversation by shutting the door.

As soon as the lawyer was out of sight, Cyrus seated Ellie in the buggy and took his place beside her. Planning his negotiations, he slapped the reins smartly and trotted the team to the church.

The preacher's voice was loud, carrying to the street where they listened to him exhorting the congregation to resist sin and temptation.

"Cyrus," Ellie said. "I know you're an important man, but the service won't end for another two hours. How are you going to get the minister to interrupt his sermon?"

"Watch and learn," Cyrus answered wryly.

The minister drove a hard bargain. The wedding cost Cyrus a roof, a new set of steps and the promise of his ass parked in a church pew once a month, but when he ushered Eleanor back through the side door she was his bride.

* * * * *

Eleanor's grandfather was a crusty old goat.

"You're Burke." Alcott's expression was sour when he looked at Cyrus. "I understand you just bribed the minister to license your relationship with my granddaughter." He turned a disgusted glance toward Eleanor.

Cyrus nodded, keeping his mouth shut and his hand away from his gun, since he couldn't shoot the old man. But he wanted to.

"Granddaughter, you'll have to come home to Hartford. There are documents of business that you need to sign to gain control of Lacey's shares in the bank."

"Any papers to be signed will be executed in Uncle Henry's office here in town after my husband and I have discussed them."

Cyrus was proud of the way she stood up to her grandfather. Alcott didn't take it so well.

"We don't have time for this nonsense. Pack your trunks, Eleanor. We're leaving."

"No." Ellie didn't waver and though she had things in hand, Cyrus added his support.

"We'll be back to town next Wednesday to look over the paperwork and sign if we like the terms. Meanwhile, Henry, explain to Mr. Alcott who he's doing business with these days." Cyrus set a course for the exit, avoiding the coming explosion.

"The problem of William's partners has been resolved, sir." Henry said. He called after them as they reached the door. "Mr. Burke, there are also some details about your bank shares we need to discuss when you have time."

"What was that all about?" Eleanor asked as soon as they were outside.

"Just a little account balancing. Henry used some of my money to wipe out the sonovabitches who dragged you through mud."

"You destroyed them?"

"Yep."

Eleanor gave him a look tinged with guilt. "I should have warned you. I think my grandfather may have sent Henry to your bank to expand the Alcott Company's reach."

"That he did," Cyrus agreed amiably. "I planned on bankrupting him too, but now that's he's kin, we'll have to parley."

Eleanor pointed at the sign Cyrus had mounted over her store. "Evidently, I'm not the only one who got my *Just Desserts*."

"I don't know if I deserve you, Ellie, but I've sure as hell got you now." Cyrus lifted her into the buggy before taking his place by her side. "Your uncle's a smart financial man. I made a lot of money driving those bastards out of business."

"Good. Remember that when you furnish my teashop," she said sedately, snuggling under his arm as she outlined the details she'd already planned.

"You've palmed your bakery off on your aunt. Who the hell's going to run a new business?"

"My sisters," she smiled sweetly, patting his knee. "I think they'll find Texas quite liberating. They're coming to live with us—all three."

"We'll negotiate," he said, settling his arm around Ellie's shoulders. As she stroked her hand up his thigh and squeezed, Cyrus flicked the reins, driving like hell toward home.

Epilogue

"Phoebe is a so intelligent, Cyrus. She's joined the Hartford Historical Society and spends hours at the library. Grandfather fears she's in danger of becoming a bluestocking."

Cyrus listened to Ellie describe her sisters for the hundredth time that day.

"Augusta can fix any mechanical device. She's been plaguing Grandfather to visit France so she can inspect a self-propelled vehicle housed in a museum there."

"And your other sister?" From Ellie's descriptions, Cyrus was expecting three prim and proper misses, rigidly moral members of the cult of true womanhood, just as Eleanor had been before he got his hands on her.

He studied her. She looked…happy. He sure as hell was. He'd do just about anything to keep things going good.

"I can't wait for you to meet Josephine. She's a talented artist. I've asked her to bring her paints and create a lovely landscape for us while she's here."

Ellie had obviously missed her family more than she'd let on. He was bringing the girls to Texas for a while, the *while* part being undetermined. He'd asked Ellie a couple of times but somehow the conversation always turned to other things, so his recollection of when they were leaving was somewhat vague.

Old Man Alcott had seemed eager to send them on their way and Ellie's uncle didn't have much at all to say about their visit. Recently, though, Henry had been wearing a perpetual look of worry. Cyrus had an uneasy feeling he wouldn't like why, but unless Henry saw fit to share, whatever the problem was, it didn't concern Cyrus.

Over a month ago Henry and his wife, Millie, attended Sunday dinner at the Burke ranch. After he'd eaten two pieces of Ellie's pecan pie, and had his cup filled with coffee twice, Henry put down his napkin and announced, "Eleanor, thanks to your husband, Mr. Burke, your accusers have been revealed as scoundrels."

Cyrus felt a twitch of pride at that. He'd ordered Henry Alcott to go after the assholes financially and in every other way. Ellie's uncle had been on 'em like a Bluetick scenting game. Hell, the miscreants never had a chance.

He'd made a pile of money from ruining the bastards, but that paled next to the way Ellie looked when Henry shared the news. If he lived to be a hundred and five, Cyrus would never forget the way her eyes had shone with unshed tears and she'd gazed at him like he was a goddamned wonder.

Regardless of company present, she'd leaned close to him and whispered, "Cyrus Burke, I love you more than Friday night baths." And his britches had gotten too tight remembering their last foray in the tub upstairs.

It had occurred to Cyrus, that if Ellie was pining for anything back East, now that she'd been found innocent of all the ugly accusations flying around, she might be considering a visit to her former home. So he decided to bring the Alcott sisters to Texas and nip that impulse in the bud.

Eleanor Alcott-Burke—her grandfather had insisted on the Alcott addition—and damned if Cyrus hadn't agreed when Ellie had whispered, "Please." Cyrus understood that his bride had a family she loved. He wasn't about to make her regret staying on the ranch with him.

The train to Paris, Texas should have arrived a half hour earlier but delays weren't uncommon. He'd brought the buckboard to haul the girls' fiddle-faddle to the ranch, and Ellie was beside herself with plans for their visit.

If that didn't prove how much he wanted to please his woman, nothing ever would. More than one of the boys had hunkered close to ask, "Well, how is it?"

And, he always answered the same. "Marriage to Ellie? Better than her best dessert."

"Shit," they'd say, and walk away, hungry for a woman of their own.

Good. Then they'd leave off looking at his wife. He'd hired a cook, built an addition onto the bunkhouse, and installed a kitchen out there just so he could keep her in the ranch house and away from their lecherous eyes.

He sighed. He'd had it good for better than two months. Aside from the mandated regular visit to the local church, things had been fine. Cyrus rested in bed every night with Ellie exhausted and purring like a kitten beside him. He slept pretty well himself.

Last night she'd worshipped his body with her mouth, using her tongue in innovative ways. He shifted on the wagon seat, adjusting his shaft as it also remembered and responded accordingly. Cyrus put his hand on Ellie's thigh and squeezed.

She turned her head and smiled, lighting up his life. With a sly grin and the dart of her tongue over her sinfully sweet lips, she assured him she remembered last night too.

He could have drowned in that look and stayed down all day. But the train chugged into the depot and Ellie bounced on the seat like a little girl. She started to scramble from the wagon.

"Best stay up top with me. You can look over the crowd and find 'em from here faster."

Her expression bordered on mutinous until Henry and Millie arrived in the nick of time to solve that issue. For some unknown reason, they'd carted Mable Smyth along in their back seat.

Cyrus let Henry hurry through the people milling on the crowded platform. The place was teeming with folks trying to get on board and other folks getting off the train.

There was no point in him going to meet the passengers since the girls didn't know him from Adam. And there was no way in hell he'd let Ellie push and shove her way to them. As a matter of fact, he'd never seen the depot this busy.

"Henry will find them, rest assured, Eleanor. I am looking forward to meeting the dear girls. You've spoken of them so highly." Millie had curled her hair and put on more finery than usual, so Cyrus could tell she considered this a big occasion.

Good. Cyrus intended to pass a lot of the entertaining over to Millie. Between their aunt and the new tea shop, he planned for the girls' visit to be smooth, entertaining, and end quickly. Then he'd have Eleanor Alcott-Burke to himself again.

"There they are," Ellie shouted, waving her lace hanky in the air.

And an odd thing happened. The train station quieted, and the jostling men who'd been crowding the platform, all turned in the direction she pointed.

Cyrus leaned forward, staring hard at two of the cowboys who looked suspiciously like his ranch hands. Hell. They were. And damned if that wasn't Sage Beckett across the way.

"What in blazes…"

227

"It never hurts to advertise," Mable muttered and let out a cackle loud enough to make him wince. "I may have mentioned to a few customers at the store that Mrs. Burke's *unmarried* sisters would be arriving today."

"And I said a word or two about my visitors when we went to church two Sundays ago," Ellie admitted, a sparkle in her eye.

"I've instructed Henry to make a list of all the eligible bachelors in the area. As you should as well, Cyrus. You have a greater reach. We'll need your assistance."

"I need to what?" he growled at Henry's wife.

"We'll meet and vet all the men with the making of the first match. The second and third will be much easier since we'll know already who to pursue."

Cyrus resisted the urge to jump from his wagon and flee on foot. Managed. He was being managed by two, no, make that three, women. And if he wasn't mistaken, Henry had three more in tow, ushering them his way.

"Are you all right, Cyrus?" Eleanor leaned closer and gazed at him from those pretty lavender eyes he never got enough of. Her sweet expression was filled with concern.

"Fine. I'm wonderful." Never mind that he had to choke out the words. Hell no, he wasn't all right.

But, then again, maybe he was. The way she said his name made him feel warm inside. Loved.

Cyrus brushed his lips over Ellie's forehead, getting a last taste of her before her sisters staked their claim. He slid his arm around her waist, holding her close as they stood in the wagon and watched Henry escort the three Alcott misses their way.

Yep, prim and proper. Cyrus sighed. He just hoped Ellie wouldn't decide to lady-up as well.

Then Henry lost control of the situation as one girl broke away from the sedate trio, picked up her skirts, and began to run. In less than a moment, all three raced flat out across the train platform, whooping like banshees and bellowing at the top of their lungs.

"Ellie. We're here!"

The End

Cowboy Burn, a Smoke, Inc. Excerpt.

Blurb: Five days after Christmas, when the bills are pouring in and the joy's already escaped, Harley-Jane Arthur has a plan. Use her artistic talent as entertainment at an upscale kids' party, make enough money to pay January utilities, and maybe have some cash left over for her barn roof repairs. After that, she'll buy a bottle of Red and toast New Year's Eve as usual — alone.

But... after she leaves for the party, the balmy weather turns to rain, which turns to sleet, then ice, then snow. Janie's stuck in a blizzard with no trains, planes, or Uber. Then her luck changes. While trying to grab a taxi, she unwittingly sees a murder, after which she skids on her cheap boots that have no purchase, down an icy road, landing in a heaping pile of love.

Gable Matthews, a.k.a. Cowboy, has been waiting patiently these last few years for Harley-Jane to wake up from grieving for her husband.
When she's stranded during a snowstorm, he figures this might be his chance to get her attention.

Snowbound together, Gable and Janie discover passion hot enough to melt the ice. But nothing comes easy for them. There's an unpredictable snow storm, a wonky furnace, and a taxi-cab-stealing killer, all trying to interfere with their love.

Chapter One

Yes, that's me making that noise, starving artist, Harley-Jane Arthur. I tried to quiet the impolite rumble of my stomach but it wasn't cooperating. I'd passed on the cake earlier for fear I'd smear icing on my work. I regretted it now.

"Thank you so much. I think Carlie will agree, you've made this an unforgettable party." John Carson, my employer for the day, helped me into my coat after handing me a plump envelope.

"We wanted something unique. And you made it so." Laura Carson, mother of the birthday girl, enthused over the day's events.

Though I wanted to count the money before I shoved it in my pocket, being relatively couth, I tried to concentrate on the parents instead.

"It's always hard to come up with something special for birthdays between Christmas and New Year's Eve," I agreed.

"You are more than welcome to stay. The girls

233

would love it."

I had to suppress a shudder. I'd just spent three hours entertaining a dozen ten-year-olds, many of whom had parents who'd elected to leave the kids for a sleepover rather than brave the storm.

Staying was not an option.

To get away from the pre-adolescent mania, I'd walk if I had to. But, hopefully that wouldn't be necessary. I frowned down at new faux leather boots I'd worn when I'd not been expecting the balmy fifty-five degree weather to turn into a winter blizzard.

Evidently, neither had the weather forecasters. The icy whiteout had caught everyone unprepared. I peered outside the window at the street that looked more like a sheet of glass every moment.

"Thanks for the offer, but you won't have to find a corner for me. I called an Uber driver and he's on his way. He'll get me to the T-Line." I admit, I actually felt desperate as I watched for a glimpse of the car.

"Well," Laura offered hesitantly. "The forecasters are now calling for more wind and snow. I doubt if the train will be running much longer."

"Then I'd better hurry," I muttered. I spotted a car valiantly laboring up the street and hurried away from the window.

"Carlie and her friends will always remember today because of you. Thank you so much." Laura walked me to the door still oozing praise. I hoped she'd tell all her friends.

Inside my right glove, my fingers ached from three hours of non-stop pencil grasping. The envelope in my pocket made every moment worthwhile.

Five hundred dollars, twenty-five sketches, one per girl, one each of Carlie and friend, and one group picture I'd transfer to canvas and paint when I arrived home.

"You have a great New Year," drifted after me as I stepped into the cold and heard the door click shut behind me. I immediately doubted my decision.

"It is ffffreezing out here," I complained to no one. Just as well I didn't intend it for ears. The wind took that moment to shift directions, blast me with ice shards, and smack me in the face with my own words.

Before I stepped from shelter, I pulled my phone out and called for backup.

"Looks like I might be late getting home tonight, Kenny. Can I get you to do my chores?" Cell service faded in and out as I begged my neighbor for help and received confirmation my livestock would be tended.

Even over the storm, I could hear the excited conversation in the background. Then the voice at the end changed.

"Where are you? Gable's downtown. He can come and get you." Kenny's mom offered help in the form of her brother.

Cowboy Matthews to the rescue. Yippee ki-yay.

"That's not necessary," I answered quickly. "Tell Kenny I said thanks, again."

Lifting my tote, I used it to shield myself as I left the porch, stepped ankle-deep into a drift, and waded through piles of wet yuck to get to the sidewalk.

"Damn, damn, damn." With every step the new boots made it clear they weren't created for snow walking. Icy water seeped through fake leather, wetting my socks and feet. The view from the Carsons' window hadn't prepared me for this.

After I disconnected, not thirty seconds later my phone pinged. I knew the caller without checking the ID. My voice was more than a little breathless when I fumbled to answer.

"Hi, Gable. Beth said you were downtown. I'm already on my way home. I just needed Kenny's help because I'm running laaate—"

The wind chose that moment to whip around the corner and push me farther along the sidewalk. My voice wavered as I adjusted my stance, trying to find balance.

"Doesn't sound like you're on your way home. Where are you?"

"I'll be at the T-Line and on the train before you can get here. Thanks for the offer."

"The address," he growled, ignoring my refusal.

"Mount Lebanon," I answered, giving him the name of the suburb without specifics. I disconnected and faced a more immediate challenge than Gable Matthews—not freezing to death in the winter storm.

Good thing I called for a car earlier. Before I had time to shove the phone into my pocket, it chimed again. I fumbled with it, ready to tell Gable again that I didn't want a ride. He big-brother-bossed his sister around, and by extension, sometimes, me.

"Stuck downtown. Can't get up the hill to pick you up." The Uber driver delivered the bad news and disconnected.

I started to turn, intending to go back to the Carson house. Without warning, blizzard winds billowed around me, catching the canvas tote and pushing. Relentlessly, I slid down the hill, away from the birthday party and toward the train station. I managed to stop, but literally could not get back up the sidewalk. I contemplated crawling, but my feet started another downward slide before I decided.

After sleet had fallen earlier, it had coated the sidewalks and turned the streets to ice. Then, icy rain had changed to snow, covering the slippery mess with a thick, wet blanket. The wind cleared some spots, revealing the treacherous base. In other areas, snow varied from thin crusts to drifts.

"This is not good, this is not good at all," I whimpered, trying to maintain my balance on the slick surface under my feet.

A Stop sign marking the spot where two streets intersected loomed in front of me. I slammed into it, clinging to the metal pole as I tried to get my bearings. I'd never visited this gentrified suburb before today.

I'd walked from the T-Line up the street, but the houses looked a lot different under snow and ice than they had earlier in the day with their elegant holiday decorations displayed under a warm sun.

I squinted through the snow, identifying a group of people on the other side of the street. Lights suddenly cut through the storm as a taxi fishtailed its way to the curb and the huddled group lunged for the handle.

I lunged too. But before I could reach the spot, they'd all climbed inside. Whether they saw me or not was a moot point. The last one inside slammed the door and the cab took off.

"Damn, damn, damn," I muttered as the vehicle surged out of a rut and dirty snow hit me in the face.

Halfway down the block, another taxi idled in the middle of the street. Maybe my luck had changed.

"Mine," I vowed and plunged through the storm, moving in the direction of the blurry beacon on top of the car.

I slid to a halt on one side of the vehicle at the same time two figures, one man leaning heavily on another, loomed out of the storm's fury and reached for the same cab from the far side.

I attempted to jerk open the back door but a gale force wind threatened to knock me off my feet. Nevertheless, I clung to the handle, determined to get inside and stake my claim.

"I'll share," I gasped when I finally won my struggle and wrenched it open.

"No you won't." One of the men on the other side shoved his companion into the seat before I could slide inside.

I glared at both men clearly outlined by the dome light in the cab, ready to fight for space in the cab.

But the first man sprawled drunkenly all over the seat. I was ready to climb in and make room for myself anyway when the driver chimed in. "Cab's taken."

Ready to argue, I leaned in farther, but the driver accelerated, rocking his tires enough to threaten me.

I gave up, backed away, and let the force of the blizzard rip the door from my hand. Instead of climbing into his stolen ride, the second man closed his door, and rapped on the top of the taxi.

"Take off." Spinning tires and lurching heavily, the vehicle moved away, leaving me staring across the open space at the cab thief. The next gust of wind whipped the hem of his trench coat and he slid on the ice-covered pavement.

I peered through the swirling snow, uncharitably glad to see him fall on his ass. He gave me such a dark look, I had no desire to offer assistance as he began to rise.

The wind took away the decision to help him when it slammed me with enough force to send me sliding down the sloping road.

Hope there's no traffic at the bottom of the hill. I slowed my descent down the twisty, narrow road by grabbing cars that residents had parked in the street. In more than one, the security alarm blared and lights flashed, warning the homeowners that a demented artist skidded down their hill.

Once, the wind shifted and carried the sound of a man's curse. I realized that someone, probably the cab thief, followed in my tracks. That freaked me out, and instead of concentrating on keeping my balance, I tried to increase my speed, which turned out to be a mistake.

I fell, landing on the canvas tote, which acted like a sled, shooting me downward at an alarming speed until I collided with a garbage can covered in snow. I'd rounded the bend in the road before I crashed, and as I leaned on my elbows, catching my breath, I could see the lights from the T-Line in the distance.

I could also see the F-150 idling in the middle of the cross-section between streets. The door opened and a size thirteen set of boots, followed by a sinewy length of hardened steel, stepped down.

I silently willed the wind to catch Gable Matthews' trademark Stetson. But it didn't. He pulled it lower, stepped closer, and peered down at me.

"Need some help?"

"How'd you know where to find me?" I croaked, reaching up a hand so he could pry me out of the drift.

"Lights flashing and horns blaring. Knew it was you." He pulled me up and sheltered my body with his as he walked me to his truck.

I ignored his oblique reference to the time he'd deactivated my car alarm after it had blared loud enough and long enough to wake my neighbor—one of those six degrees of separation things—his sister, Beth.

I didn't miss his drawled sarcasm. But, I didn't have the breath for a snappy response left in me. Being not much more than five feet tall, it was always a struggle for me to reach the running board on the giant's truck.

This time I lost my battle to climb up. Cold had settled in my knees and I thought they might never work again.

Gable slid his arm under my legs, lifted me into the big Ford pickup, parked my fanny on his heated seat, tucked my canvas tote in the back, and shut the door before I knew what he'd planned.

Ahh... I actually moaned out loud as he jogged around to his side.

The door opened, the truck tilted toward the driver's side, and a blast of cold air accompanied Gable as he swung up and inside. As soon as he settled under the steering wheel, he handed me a towel.

I'd been melting. Water puddled around me on his leather seats. Embarrassed, I wiped my face, and tried to blot the ice from my hat. He pulled the hat off, unleashing the mess of brown hair that tumbled out and around my shoulders.

"Great, now it's wet, too," I complained.

Before I could protest, he gathered it in his

hand, pulled it away from my face, and squinted down at me. "Mud, I think." He brushed my cheek with his thumb. "You been playin' in a dirt pile?"

"I've been earning money for a new barn roof," I muttered stiffly, reaching for my hat.

"Your hair's a mite damp. Best let it dry." He laid my knit cap out of reach on the dashboard closer to the heat. "Mind telling me why you're skating around up here in a blizzard?"

Beth laughed at Gable's tendency to micromanage anything he involved himself in. Sometimes he forgot I wasn't his sister and tried to boss me as well. Apparently, this was one of those times.

"Kids' party. I was the entertainment. The mud's from the tires of a taxi I tried to chase down." I shut up, then thought of more explanation.

"And if you'll recall, it was fifty-five degrees this morning." I decided I'd better tone down my indignation since he'd come out in the storm to find me. Plus, I remembered I had to get home. "You can just drop me at the train station," I murmured.

"Quit running a half hour ago."

"Oh." That sounded dumb. I didn't know what to say. I didn't want to ask him to drive to the country. The wind whistled and roared around the truck, sounding more like a locomotive than a storm. Home seemed farther away each moment.

I shivered inside my wet coat. Gable muttered a curse, cranked up the heat, turned on some music, and put the truck in gear.

I closed my eyes and enjoyed being out of the cold. There was no reason to ask where we were going. We'd go wherever Cowboy Matthews wanted to go. My eyes popped open again when I remembered the other stranded pedestrian.

"There was a man behind me. We were both on foot." I waved toward the street where snow already covered my skid marks.

Gable honked his horn and backed the truck around enough to shine his lights up the narrow roadway. I couldn't see anything.

When nobody appeared, he sighed, put the engine back in park, took a flashlight with a megawatt beam from the back seat, and climbed out.

My gaze followed the light as he walked away. Whether it was Gable disappearing into whiteout or the howl of the wind making me shudder, I waited tense and worried inside the truck. I thought about the cab thief and why he was on foot. We both could have been in the taxi and not on foot. I didn't like the idea of Gable alone out there looking for a fool.

I knew he was freezing his tail off since I'd just been out there. Darn it. I gnawed my lip, wondering what I should do. I just wanted to curl up on the leather seat and…

I drifted, thawing into a muddle of thoughts, one of them wondering if I should climb out and join the hunt. The slam of the truck door jarred me awake.

"Nobody up the first or second street. I yelled.

Don't know if they'd have heard, but they would have seen my light."

The heater inside the cab had steadily kicked out heat, making me toasty warm. I stared blearily up at him. Yep, still had his hat on. But, he used a moment to take it off and toss it in the back.

He brushed his hand over his military-short burr and met my glance with his own obsidian gaze. I looked away first.

"You all right?"

Gable's rumbled question vibrated through my body, sending warning signals along with something else to my brain. The console I'd been leaning against disappeared, leaving me propped against a hard body instead.

"I'm okay." I gave no notice to the arm curled around my shoulders and concentrated on the sweep of the wipers chasing ice across the glass.

"I'll watch," I mumbled. I intended to stay alert and be a help to the driver.

"Suit yourself. But first, rest a minute, let your

body know you're safe." He hitched me closer, until I felt his heat from thigh to shoulder. Then he snapped my seatbelt in place and angled my head against his chest. I inhaled his scent and closed my eyes. *Just for a moment...*

End of Excerpt

From the Author

Hi. I'm Gem Sivad. I live in in the southern part of an enchanted kingdom where I enjoy the slow pace of life that gives me time to study the world and imagine incredible adventures.

My sexy, gritty romances, usually contain more than a pinch of naughty and definitely include a splash of fun.

Although I have hermit tendencies, occasionally I come out of the writer's den to meet readers at book signing events. Hope to see you there. But in case we miss each other, you can find me at the cyber locations below.

For book release updates (or if you're an avid Words with Friends junkie like I am) hang out with me on Facebook @: facebook.com/GemSivadAuthor. Visit the Gem Sivad website @ gemsivad.com for snippets from the current works in progress. And of course, by subscribing to Dreamcatcher newsletter@ http://gemsivad.com/subscribe/ you'll never miss a Gem Sivad contest or giveaway.

Nice meeting you,
Gem Sivad

More Books by Gem Sivad

Historical Westerns
Unlikely Gentlemen series:
River's Edge
Outrageous Pride
Cerise Amour

Eclipse Heat series:
Quincy's Woman
Perfect Strangers
Wolf's Tender
Tupelo Gold
Five Card Stud
Breed True
Trouble in Disguise
Whispering Grace

Historical Paranormal
Jinx series:
Cat Nip
Blood Stoned

Contemporary Paranormal
Bitter Creek Holler series:

Call Me Miz
Miz Spelled
Ursus Horribilis

Contemporary Romantic Suspense
Smoke, Inc. series
Cowboy Burn
Rhythm

44514915R00150

Printed in Poland
by Amazon Fulfillment
Poland Sp. z o.o., Wrocław